Dear Reader,

It is with great delight and joy that I wrote
What Family Means, my second published novel,
for you. Set in my native city of Buffalo, New York,
and the surrounding western New York area, this
story demonstrates what love of one another and
love for family can do. It can bridge backgrounds,
communities, people from all walks of life. In
the not-too-distant past heroes and heroines
from different backgrounds and upbringings
weren't applauded when they fell in love, or when
they managed to make their love work despite
overwhelming odds against it. Will Bradley and
Debra Schaefer not only made it through the
struggles and conflicts that their families and
society threw at them, they raised a beautiful family.
And their love still endures after almost forty years
of marriage.

I hope you are able to cheer on both Debra and
Will as they face their conflicts, yesterday's and
today's, to provide a love that lasts a lifetime, not
just for them as a couple but for their family. *Love*,
this is what family means.

Please send me your thoughts on this story via my
Web site, www.gerikrotow.com.

Peace,

Geri Krotow

WHAT FAMILY MEANS
Geri Krotow

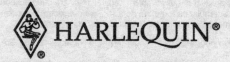

HARLEQUIN®

TORONTO • NEW YORK • LONDON
AMSTERDAM • PARIS • SYDNEY • HAMBURG
STOCKHOLM • ATHENS • TOKYO • MILAN • MADRID
PRAGUE • WARSAW • BUDAPEST • AUCKLAND

Recycling programs
for this product may
not exist in your area.

ISBN-13: 978-0-373-71547-3
ISBN-10:   0-373-71547-1

WHAT FAMILY MEANS

www.eHarlequin.com

Printed in U.S.A.

ABOUT THE AUTHOR

Raised in Buffalo and western New York State, Geri always dreamed of romance and adventure. A graduate of the U.S. Naval Academy, she moves around the world with her navy pilot husband, two children, a dog and a parrot. Geri loves to hear from readers. You can reach her at her Web site, www.gerikrotow.com.

Books by Geri Krotow

HARLEQUIN EVERLASTING LOVE
20–A RENDEZVOUS TO REMEMBER

With all my love to Alex and Ellen,
who teach me every day what family means.

CHAPTER ONE

Present Day
Buffalo, New York
Debra

"YOU'VE NEVER BELIEVED ME about this the whole time we've been married. Why should I expect you to change now?"

Will Bradley, my husband of thirty-five years, stared at me with an intensity that made my hands clench on the shirt I was putting in his suitcase. His charcoal eyes sparked with annoyance. Will was never one to get easily worked up, but judging by the twitch over his left eyebrow, my latest obsession with our grown children's lives had sent him over the edge.

Or at least very close to it.

"I hear you, Will, you know I do. But the kids, especially Angie, haven't had the smoothest path."

I tried to keep the "look" off my face—the expression Will and our children said I'd mastered. The "I'm right so don't even bother to argue" look.

Apparently I didn't succeed in keeping my face blank. Will's nostrils flared as he drew a deep breath.

"Dammit, Debra, you go back to this every time." Will referred to my long-held belief—and, okay, *guilt*—that our interracial marriage had placed undue burden on our children.

He glanced up from packing.

"What do you always say to me, Deb? 'It's the twenty-first century. The new generation doesn't see us in terms of skin color. We don't get a fraction of the stares we used to draw.'"

"Give me some credit, Will. I know that times have changed, and the kids are all doing great—better than a lot of our friends' children."

I stood up from the bed to make my point.

"Angie's always had it the toughest. She's older than the twins and remembers the more-blatant prejudice in high school and college. Jesse's family wasn't immediately supportive of their white son marrying our biracial daughter."

Will didn't respond as he packed his socks and underwear. I hated when he went all quiet like this.

"Why did Angie move back to Buffalo while Jesse's away? Why didn't she wait for him to return from his mission?"

I knew I wasn't the only one worried about Jesse's safety in Iraq, where he'd gone for humanitarian reasons. He was there to use his surgical skills, working as a government contractor. The military was grateful for civilian talent such as Jesse's.

Will ran a hand over his short-cropped hair. His fingers caught my eyes. I was always a sucker for his hands—chocolate-brown skin stretched over the most elegant fingers, the most sensual hands, I've ever seen. He could have been a doctor like his father if he'd wanted to. But his passion was architecture. He'd used those fingers to produce beautiful buildings instead.

"This is what *I've* never understood, Will. How can you be angry with me for caring about our children?"

"There's a big difference between caring and care-*taking*, Debra."

"Don't *I* know it." As soon as the words slipped out, I realized they would've been better kept unspoken.

I sounded like a first-class martyr.

Will's hands rested on his still-slim hips, his stance combative.

"Is *that* what this is about? Do you need a break? I know it's been a long year for you, Deb." Will referred to my looking after his elderly mother, Violet. She'd become more dependent on us the past nine months.

He didn't give me a chance to answer.

"I'd be home more if I could," he went on, "but I need to take care of these last projects, then I'll go down to just a few a year, let Blair and my associates run things." Will zipped up his suitcase as I watched from my perch on our bed.

It was a ritual we'd shared since the early days of our marriage. I brought in the piles of clean laundry, he chose what he needed for his business trips, and we talked while he packed.

We usually didn't fight.

"Honey," I said now, "I don't want to argue. I just want to be here for Angie. And I'd love to have your support."

"I know, baby, she's your only daughter." Will smiled at me despite his anger at my too-familiar behavior.

I sighed.

Will walked around to my side of the bed.

"The twins were much more difficult when they were younger," I said. "Now that they're grown, it's as though they don't need their mama so much. They're men. But Angie—a daughter always needs her mother." I couldn't help the tear that slid out from under my closed lid as Will pulled me into his embrace.

"Honey, I'm just asking you to focus more on yourself, on *us*. You've given Angie and the boys the childhood, the family, you never had and we're richer for it."

I soaked up his love, but the question that wouldn't die nagged at my conscience.

Had it really been enough?

April 11, 1957
Buffalo, New York

SOMETIME AFTER THREE, the school bus churned to a stop in front of the clapboard house. Debra knew the house; it signaled the end of her half day of kindergarten. She was in Miss May's afternoon class at Lakeview Elementary. Debra liked riding to school on the noon bus because there were only five-year-olds with her. But in the afternoons the older kids came on, all the way up to fourth grade. She thought some of the boys were scary and did her best to sit with her friends.

She got off the bus with four other children. Linda and Lori, twins with matching everything from their blond braids to their saddle shoes, walked to the right and headed toward their duplex.

"Come on." Will tugged at Debra's jacket sleeve.

Debra stared at the older boy who ordered her around.

Will. Her mother told her this morning just to go home with him. Debra didn't like it that she couldn't go to her own house and be there with Mommy. But Daddy had been gone a long time, and Mommy said they needed grocery money.

So Mommy, who quit nursing school when she met Daddy and had Debra, got herself a job at the doctor's down the street.

Mommy said the doctor hired her because she needed a job and he didn't care what color her skin was. Besides, Mommy said she was the best receptionist around and Dr. Bradley knew it.

Dr. Bradley was Will's daddy.

Will was several steps ahead of her before he turned around.

"Are you coming?"

He seemed so big. He was in the second grade and had homework every night. She brought home her crayon drawings but she'd seen Will's big-boy artwork. He'd even made a round blue ball one day, painted like a globe.

Debra heard him tell another boy it was "papier-mâché." She didn't know what papier-mâché was but couldn't wait to get old enough to do her own papier-mâché.

Will sure must be smart.

"Coming." She forced her sneakered feet to walk faster. She'd never played with Will, even though they rode the same bus and his house was just one block from hers.

Will was Colored, and Mommy said Debra needed to play with girls her "own age." But Debra figured that her "own age" also meant her "own color." None of their family had the same skin color as Will.

Will looked like Gladys in third grade, who rode their bus, too. But they were the only two dark-skinned kids Debra knew who attended Lakeview Elementary.

She found it strange that Mommy hadn't let her play with Will before but now it was okay to go to his house. She didn't ask Mommy about it, though. Mommy was busy with work.

They got to the top of the steps at Will's house. Will looked at her with the nicest brown eyes she'd ever seen.

"Here you go. Your mama's inside."

Fear twisted her tummy.

"But where are *you* going?" He wasn't leaving her alone here, was he?

"Home."

Tears welled up in her eyes and she scrubbed at them with the back of her hand. Her hand had freckles, but Will's was smooth and a rich dark brown that reminded her of the chocolate frosting on her favorite doughnut. The kind with the pink sprinkles.

"But this *is* your home, Will. My mommy said to go home with *you*."

"This is my father's office. Our house is round back." He jerked his thumb over his shoulder.

Her bottom lip shook and she tried to be brave and keep her chin still.

Will sighed. A big-boy sigh.

"I'll take you in." His voice sounded mad, but he put his arm around her shoulders and guided her through the front door, which he opened with his other arm.

Debra decided Will wasn't so bad, after all. They stepped together into the front parlor. Debra saw lots of folks, mostly Colored like Will, sitting in chairs and on sofas around the room.

"There you are, pumpkin! Come on back. Thanks, William." Mommy was sitting behind a counter and still had her suit on.

"You're welcome, Mrs. Schaefer."

William left then, and the warmth of his arm around her was gone.

"Hi, Mommy." She stood at the back of the counter with her mom.

Mommy leaned down and kissed her cheek.

"Listen, sweetheart, Mommy has to work for a couple more hours. There's a little chair and table for you, see?" She pointed at the corner, where it was set up, kind of like in Debra's classroom.

"Okay, Mommy." Debra unzipped her jacket and hung it on the back of the chair like she saw grown-ups do. She could work just like Mommy but on her drawings. If she stayed quiet, she knew Mommy could work longer and earn more money for groceries. Last time they went to the grocery store, Mommy didn't have enough money for cereal. "Bread goes further, Debra," she'd said. "We can have toast in the morning and sandwiches for supper."

But Debra hadn't been able to take her eyes off the

bright cereal boxes, with pictures of the prizes inside. Maybe this time Mommy would have enough for the cereal with the rabbit on the box.

CHAPTER TWO

Present Day
Buffalo, New York

WILL PULLED the vibrating cell phone out of his pocket. He cast a quick glance at his watch. He had plenty of time before his flight left Buffalo International for L.A.

"Hi, Angie. What's going on with my favorite daughter?"

"Hey, Daddy." He visualized Angie rolling her eyes as she grinned wryly, the way she always did when he referred to her as his "favorite daughter." She was his only daughter, and he never got tired of yanking her chain, even if she was thirty-five and he was fifty-nine.

"Is this a bad time?"

"No." He shoved his papers into his briefcase. "I'm getting ready to leave on a trip. Your mom beat me out the door today—she's got a lot to do."

"I know, and I'm thrilled for her." A pause, not usual for his loquacious daughter. "I need to talk to you, Dad."

Uh-oh. It was a serious, adult-Angie topic.

"Shoot."

"I'm going to talk to Mom later today." He heard her voice tremble, and wondered what the deal was.

"Okay." He silently braced himself.

"Jesse doesn't know I want to stay here permanently. We're...having some problems, Dad."

"What?" The cogs clicked. He'd thought it odd that they hadn't purchased a home when Angie landed a job with the local weather station; he'd also wondered why they hadn't mentioned the specific job Jesse, a gifted neurosurgeon, would take here in Buffalo.

The biggest clue he'd overlooked was the fact that Angie had rented an apartment. She'd said that she and Jesse would "find a house later."

"No. Yes, well, partly." Evasiveness wasn't a typical trait of Angie's and her behavior wasn't doing much to ease his concern.

"Just spit it out, Angie."

"I'm not sure we're going to make it, Dad."

Will waited, holding his breath.

"Jesse's great. It's nothing he's done but sometimes it's really hard, with the two careers and everything."

"You two have always worked it out before, Angie. I'm confident this won't be any different." Will knew his words sounded too businesslike but he also knew that if he pushed Angie too hard, she'd clam up and not ask for help when she really needed it. Besides, Angie was meeting with Debra later today. Angie would give Deb the details, and Deb would share them with Will.

"Thanks, Dad. Did you and Mom ever have problems like this?"

"Honey bunny, I don't know what particular problems you're having, but, yes, we've had our ups and downs. Every marriage does. We were blessed with a strong love early on. But when we decided to give it a run, well, we've told you kids what we went through."

"I know, Dad." Of the three kids, Angie had taken the brunt of the racism and prejudice faced by their young family. But that was more than thirty years ago. Angie had grown into an intelligent, beautiful woman with a mind of her own.

"If you want me, I'll come over later this week, when I'm back from my trip, sweetheart." He'd helped her unpack a few days earlier, and hung some pictures on the walls of her tiny apartment.

"No, that's okay, Dad. With the weather this time of year, there's no telling when I'll get home at night."

"It *is* Buffalo in February." He was grateful for the heated interior of his SUV.

"Talk to you later, Dad." She paused. "Dad? Thanks for being here for me, not just today, but all the time."

"I'm honored to be here for you, Angie."

And he was. Nothing made Will prouder than his family.

December 1958
Buffalo, New York

"ARE YOU SURE it's okay for us to come in here?"

Debra's bottom was still sore from the spanking she got from Mommy last night. She and Will had been in the woods, out of sight of the front office. Mommy had been scared when she couldn't see Debra.

The spanking wasn't that bad, not as hard as Daddy's were with the belt when he'd been drinking. But the sharp sting of Mommy's hand told her she wasn't ever to do that again.

Or at least not to let Mommy *know* she was playing in the woods with Will. Every so often, Debra circled back to the swing set in the grassy area behind the office building. That way, if Mommy looked out the window she'd see her.

"Shh, we're fine. Your mother has another couple hours of work. Didn't you see all those folks in the waiting room?"

Will always had the answers, and Debra trusted him. He was the big brother she wished she had. Her rag doll that Aunt Jenna made her was okay, but it wasn't Will. She loved her doll but it was still scary in the dark corners of her room.

She followed Will's steps up the winding path that went so far she couldn't see the end. They walked through the woods behind the playground for a long, long time.

"Will, I'm not sure 'bout this. It's gonna get dark soon."

Their breath formed crystal balloons in front of their faces, and the ground crackled with early winter frost. In two weeks it would be Christmas.

"Just another little bit, Deb, and we'll be there."

She liked how he called her "Deb" instead of "Debra." It made her feel smart and more like a big girl.

"Okay, Will." She shuffled her red rubber boots through some blackened leaves and kept up with him.

Will was right. In a few minutes they came out of the woods and onto a huge lawn. Even with the onset of winter, it was the greenest grass Debra had ever seen. Looming over them was a giant house.

"Will, is that a castle?" she whispered, afraid her outdoor voice would ruin the vision.

Will laughed. She liked how he laughed. It was like a giggle with no end, and his white teeth were so bright against his skin.

"That's no castle, Deb, that's my house. C'mon, let's go inside."

But her feet didn't want to move. Mommy wouldn't be happy that she'd gone inside Dr. Bradley's house. He was Mommy's boss. And Will's family was Colored. Debra was pretty sure she wasn't supposed to go into a Colored person's house.

Will turned back when he got to the front door, and from the distance she saw his scowl.

"Aww, Deb, let's go! It's cold out here. Don't you want a snack?"

Debra's stomach growled when he said "snack." It was always such a long time until supper.

"I'm comin'. Just wait." She hurried toward him, her boots crunching on the frost-tipped lawn.

She reached his side and Will grinned at her.

"What?" She held out her mittened hands. Was he going to make fun of her freckles like the other boys did?

"You look like a fairy princess, Deb. Just pretend this is your castle."

"Okay, Will."

He opened the door and Debra followed close behind. She didn't want to be left alone, either outside or in the huge house they'd entered.

They stepped into a room that made her think of the movies. A winding staircase in painted white wood wound up, up, to a landing way over their heads. A table with the biggest vase was directly in front of them. She wondered why there weren't any flowers in this vase. Why have a vase if you don't have flowers?

"Will, is that you?" A soft female voice floated down from above.

"Yes, Mama."

He glanced at Debra and put his finger on his lips. He didn't have to, though. Debra couldn't have squeaked out a single syllable. She was afraid she'd pee her pants, she was so scared.

Would Will's mama be mad at them for coming in?

"I'm up here feeding your brother. There are cookies on the counter, but don't eat more than two."

"Yes, Mama." Will smiled at Debra and grabbed her hand.

"See? It's okay! Let's go get a cookie!" His voice wasn't a complete whisper but it was quieter than she was used to.

She trailed him into a small passageway and then through a swinging door into a kitchen like none she'd ever seen. Huge pots and pans hung from the ceiling and there was a long wooden table in the middle of the room. Debra counted eight chairs.

"We don't have eight chairs in our whole house, Will."

"Who cares, Deb? Here, have a cookie."

He handed her a big oatmeal raisin cookie and she took a bite. It was delicious!

"Where does your mom buy these?"

Will snorted.

"She doesn't buy them. Patsy bakes them for us."

"Who's Patsy?"

"Our help. Don't you have help at your house?"

"No. But it's just me and Mommy, so we don't need help."

"Oh."

They slid into the high cane chairs and continued to munch on their cookies. Debra couldn't stop looking at the kitchen.

The tall cupboards had frosted glass on them and she could see stacks of dishes. When did Will's family ever use so many dishes? She wondered if he had his own dish, like her plate with the cartoon moose on it. Probably not.

Will was a big boy already.

"Will, did you—"

The voice reached Debra's ears and jolted her upright. She turned and faced Will's mommy.

Violet Bradley was so pretty, wrapped in a soft pink bathrobe. She even wore fuzzy pink slippers to match. And the little baby she held was so tiny! Had Debra and Will been that tiny? What would it be like to have a brother or sister?

"Will! You didn't tell me you had a guest."

From Violet's tone Debra knew that Will was in trouble. And from the flash in his mother's eyes, she knew it was *her* fault. She'd gotten Will into trouble. Debra felt a sick feeling in her tummy.

"This is Deb. Her mom works in Daddy's office." Will stood straight in front of his mom and Debra was glad he was there, glad they were facing Mrs. Bradley together.

"I know who she is, Will, but why is she here?"

"I had to go to the potty." Debra remembered the *I Love Lucy* shows she watched with Mommy, where the friends were always sticking up for each other. So she stuck up for Will.

"There's a bathroom in the office," Will's mother replied but still didn't look at her. She was staring hard at Will, though. Debra wished she'd never agreed to come home with Will.

"But it's cold, Mom, and you have the best cookies." Even Violet couldn't resist such charm.

She sighed. "You take two cookies each and go back to the office right away. The girl's mother will worry."

"Thanks, Mom."

"Thank you, Mrs. Bradley." Debra slipped through the kitchen door as quickly and quietly as she could.

Violet's reply followed her into the foyer.

"Will, after you take her back, you come straight home. Do you understand me, Will?"

"Yes, Mama."

CHAPTER THREE

Present Day
Buffalo, New York
Debra

THE SCREAM LODGED in the back of my throat. I swallowed and bit my lip. I no longer viewed the knitting needles in my hands as tools that turned a hand-spun mohair blend into a piece of art.

They were potential weapons.

If I heard one more boring remark about family trees from any of the ladies seated around the café table, I was going for it.

I was going to poke my eyes out.

"I like knitting, but it's not the same as scrapbooking." Shirley sat across the table from me and went on to rave about how scrapbooking had changed her life.

I wasn't convinced. "Shirley, that's nice, but isn't it a lot of work, clipping and gluing and finding the right colored papers?"

Our group's youngest member at age thirty-four, Maggie paged through Shirley's latest creation. Her slim hand turned another sheet of Shirley's ode to her youngest grandchild.

"I agree. Give me a ball of good yarn and my rosewood needles and I'm set for any journey." Dolores laughed. She was her own best audience.

Nine of us sat at the restaurant table, our breakfast dishes long cleared. We'd met here every Wednesday morning for the past several years. To knit, talk and grouse.

Maybe I could steer the conversation back to knitting.

"I just think it'd be tough to go through every single photo I've ever taken." I kept purling as I spoke. "Besides, the best time of my life is *now*. I love to look at baby pictures of my kids, but to have to sift through them all…"

I shuddered at the thought of the boxes and boxes of photos shoved under the eaves in our attic.

"Can anyone help me with this? I dropped a stitch rows ago but I can't bear to rip this out now." Maggie held up the wool sweater she was making for her husband. It was a beautiful cable pattern. But an ugly ladder ran down one of the cables.

"Let me show you how to fix that." I stood up to walk over to her when my cell phone rang.

"Hang on." I reached into my purse and pulled out my phone.

It was Violet, my mother-in-law.

"Hey, Vi."

"Debra." Her voice was soft, too soft.

"What's wrong?"

Alarm made my simmering estrogen flush turn into an all-out hot flash. I started fanning my face with a knitting pattern.

"My legs are swollen again and I'm having a hard time moving around."

"Did you take your pills this morning?" Vi had chronic congestive heart disease. At eighty-five she was doing pretty well but every now and then her symptoms flared, despite the medications.

"Yes, but the cold's making my bones ache." I heard her sigh and the resignation it carried. Vi was used to good days and bad, but the "bad" days seemed to be getting worse, as though her circulatory system was wearing out.

And with it, her desire to continue the fight.

"I'll be home in a few minutes. Keep the phone with you." I put the phone back in its purse pocket and gathered up my knitting, shoving the needles into the large ball of yarn.

"I'm sorry, Maggie, I have to go. Can you get someone else to help?"

At Maggie's murmured agreement, I finished my cup of tea.

"Debra, of all people, *you* should put together a series of scrapbooks about your family. You've been through more than any of us. You're a living part of American history!" Shirley's intent gaze was on me and I saw the serious glint in her blue eyes.

I waved my hand. "Please. Let's not be drama queens. We've all had our troubles." I returned my knitting to my tapestry tote bag. I was sorry to leave and even sorrier that Vi wasn't feeling well. But I was also secretly grateful for a way out of the knitting group's current conversation.

"I have to go. Vi needs me. But let me say this." I looked at Shirley.

"I'm a fiber artist. I knit, I weave, I create. I do things for my family every day. Why take time to agonize about the past? I don't want to miss a minute of today. Anyway, I thought scrapbooking was to celebrate the *joy* of life."

Shirley didn't buy it.

"There are many ways to celebrate life and our families," she said. "But scrapbooking gives your children a history to draw from."

She was the most vocal of our group, which I'd started almost a dozen years ago. Not one local election passed that Shirley wasn't involved in, and she took up what, in my opinion, were some pretty odd causes. However, I had no argument with that as long as *I* wasn't one of them.

I swallowed a sigh.

"I *do* celebrate my family, Shirley. We have great dinners whenever we can, usually on Sundays. Angie just moved back to town. Blair and Stella are finally talking babies, and Brian is successful."

I didn't mention that Will was angry at me for being too involved with the kids. Nor did I bring up my suspicion that Angie had come home to Buffalo to distance herself from her husband. That I thought Blair and Stella were approaching their attempt to start a family more like purchasing a new car. Or that I worried that Brian was too driven in his architectural career to ever find a soul mate, much less have a family.

"Deb, you've got to admit that none of us have had to fight for our husbands or family like you."

Shirley referred to the fact that I'm white and Will is black. It's not as big a deal today. When we first met over fifty years ago, it was more than a big deal. It was a showstopper as far as relationships and marriages were concerned.

I pulled out my car keys.

"Of course we had some hard times," I said. "But at least I've known Will since we were both kids. He's been a part of my life forever. Not many spouses can claim that."

I didn't want to examine the volcano of emotions that threatened to erupt at just the idea of looking back at our past. Our present was the best yet for Will and me. I didn't want to mess with it.

I *wouldn't* mess with it.

"Come on, Debra, it couldn't have been easy back in the sixties and seventies."

No, but Paris made it all possible.

I acknowledged the errant thought but didn't share it with my friends. It was too private. Paris was the time in our lives that sustained Will and me through the storms that awaited us.

"No, it was never easy. But my kids have grown up in as normal a world as I could hope for. None of them seem to have suffered. In any event, I see no point in putting myself through any of those emotions again."

Shirley shook her head and picked up her knitting.

"I hear you, Deb, but I still think you'd gain a lot out of recording your life for your kids and your future grandkids."

I smiled.

"You may be right." I shrugged into my coat and offered my best smile to the group. "See you next week. Call me if anything really stumps you."

They often asked me for help with their knitting, since I was the only professional knitter in the group.

I loved them because we shared so much more than knitting. But this morning the sharing cut too close....

These women were special to me because they loved me for *me*. They knew I was a "famous" fiber artist but accepted me as one of them. A woman with a family she'd fight to the death for.

The wind that greeted me as I exited the coffee shop was chillier than it'd been a half hour earlier. I looked up at the steel-gray clouds that seemed close enough to touch.

"More darn snow," I mumbled to myself. Mentally I went down my to-do list: check on Violet, then spend the rest of the day in my studio preparing for my upcoming art exhibition.

I had just fastened my seat belt, hand poised to turn on the car stereo so I could listen to my favorite sixties station, when my phone buzzed again. Panic fluttered in my throat but was quelled when I saw the caller.

Angie.

"Hi, honey, everything okay?" I put her on speaker so I could back out of the parking lot.

"Um, yeah, I'm fine. How are you?"

Angie's distracted tone didn't alarm me. But her question about my well-being did. Usually her conversations were full of her latest career feats as a meteorologist, and her marriage to Jesse, the love of her life.

"I'm fine, sweetheart. What's up?"

"Mom, can you meet me at the coffee shop this morning?"

"Oh, I'd love to, but I'm just leaving the knitting group. I have to go back home and check on Vi."

"Is Grandma all right?" Angie's voice rang clear and concerned over the car speaker.

"I think so. She's not getting any younger, and she needs a little extra TLC every now and then."

"Is it her heart?"

"Honey, it's *always* her heart at this point." I turned the key in the ignition—February in Buffalo felt like Siberia. The heater cranked up as I did my best to reassure Angie that Vi was likely okay.

"I really need to talk to you, Mom." The little-girl tone was back.

"Angie, are you okay?"

"Of course. I just needed to talk. It's been a huge transition for me, you know, Mom."

"Yes, it has." She'd moved back to Buffalo from San Francisco, what, only a month ago?

"Can you call me when you're done with Grandma Vi?"

"Sure thing, sweetheart. Maybe we can meet for lunch."

"Thanks, Mom."

"Bye."

I sighed and put the phone in the compartment between the large bucket front seats. I was so thrilled to have Angie home again. I just needed Brian to move here and I'd finally have all my chicks back in the nest—or at least near it. My family around me—everything I needed for happiness.

But that was before I knew Angie had decided to

make her move alone, while Jesse was deployed to Iraq with a civilian surgical augmentation team. Before I realized that Vi's congestive heart failure was changing from chronic to acute, needing to be monitored daily.

Women's magazine pundits called us the "sandwich" generation. Still raising or supporting our children and tending to our aging parents.

I silently counted my blessings as I put the car in gear. Gratitude was my antidote to the despair that could overwhelm me when I least expected it to.

First, all our children were economically independent. Second, they all had good careers and two out of three had chosen loving partners. Third, Violet was financially taken care of, with the best possible medical care.

And most important, I had Will.

Present Day
Buffalo, New York

"HEY, HOW'S IT GOING?" Angie Bradley slid onto the stool next to her younger brother Blair's at the breakfast bar. He and his wife, Stella, had refurbished this downtown loft apartment three years ago, as newlyweds.

"Are you hungry? I've got plenty of oatmeal left." Stella smiled and Angie let the flash of her perfectly straight, white teeth send their happy energy her way. Stella was a pediatric dentist and her own smile was her best advertisement.

"No, thanks."

Stella's eyebrows rose. "Are you sure? I even have real maple syrup."

Angie laughed.

"No, thanks." That was just like Stella, to remember that Angie liked the real stuff, not some flavored corn syrup. But her stomach couldn't cope with much of anything at the moment.

"You're not on a diet, are you?" Blair was five years her junior but acted like her big brother more often than not. Like his twin, Brian, Blair had followed in their dad's footsteps and was an architect. But while Blair loved Buffalo and worked in Dad's firm, Brian had left Buffalo for a position in Denver.

Angie missed seeing both her brothers but was grateful to be facing just one of them at the moment.

"No, I'm not on a diet…" She let her voice trail off. Blair nuzzled Stella's neck.

"Knock it off, Blair," Stella said with a giggle.

"Yeah, knock it off, or get a room. Geez." Angie loved to tease her brothers.

"How's your new job?"

"Great, good. It's okay. You know, it always takes a while to get familiar with a new place."

"I'm sure they're excited to have you on the team." Stella poured coffee into a brick-red mug.

"Here—it's the morning blend from the café."

Angie looked at the mug but knew if it got too close she'd be in Blair and Stella's downstairs bathroom in ten seconds flat.

"No, uh, wait—" She shoved herself off the stool and made it to the bathroom door in six seconds, to be exact.

"Come on. Be a big girl and go 'fess up," she whispered to her pale reflection in the washroom mirror.

She walked out of the bathroom and back into the kitchen, but stayed close to the door. She couldn't handle the smell of coffee right now.

"You're pregnant!" Stella's declaration caught Angie off guard, but then she teared up and smiled at her sister-in-law.

"I am."

Blair whistled.

"Miss 'I'm-not-bringing-kids-into-this-harsh-world' is going to have a baby?"

Angie looked at Blair and Stella and felt like the most unsympathetic sister possible.

"I didn't want to tell you—I was hoping you two, um…"

"Oh, honey, don't worry about us! We've just started trying, and I *am* younger than you, you know," Stella chided Angie lovingly. "Come on over here and give us a hug!"

Angie accepted Stella's hug, and the tears spilled down her cheeks. She drew back and wiped at her face with her hands.

"Here." Stella handed her a napkin from the breakfast bar.

"Thanks." Angie sniffled. "I didn't want to tell you guys—I know you're trying, and here I go and get pregnant without even planning." Angie and Jesse had always been meticulous about birth control. She knew her ovulation cycle inside out. With the effects of top-shelf champagne and the holiday season she and Jesse had enjoyed themselves on the rug next to their Christmas tree. Without protection. She'd thought she couldn't possibly get pregnant at that particular time. The baby inside her was proof that she'd been wrong.

"My doctor says we're both perfectly healthy—it's just a matter of time." Stella put her hand on Angie's forearm. "This is so exciting! Our kids will grow up together."

Blair stood in the kitchen, staring at Angie.

"What?"

"You haven't told Mom and Dad yet, have you?"

"No, I haven't—but I will. I just haven't had time alone with them." She let the little white lie hang there. She hadn't told *Jesse* yet, but that wasn't any of her family's business, was it?

"*Wooo-wee.* Mom's going to go *nuts!* When she thought we were *thinking* about trying, she flipped— even asked if we had a nursery theme picked out."

Angie laughed.

"Mom's always in the thick of it with us, you have to admit."

"I'm not used to this. My family isn't as hands-on." Stella sipped her coffee. "Hands-on" was a polite way of describing what they often saw as Debra's overinvolvement with her kids' lives. But they all knew the reasons for it, too.

"Your mom didn't have the interracial thing to deal with." Blair looked at Stella, her dark skin a testament to her African-American heritage.

"No, but she had plenty of her own worries."

"Like you marrying me?" Blair smiled sardonically.

Stella's parents had been shocked to find out that his family was mixed—Blair and Brian both had dark skin like Stella. But they'd taken it in stride.

"Knock it off, tough guy." Stella swatted Blair on the arm.

"Mom loves us, and she'd be hurt if she heard us talking like this." Angie felt a need to defend her mother. "I'll tell her to give us some space."

"Yeah, tell her to focus on Brian."

"She can't, he's in Colorado."

"Yeah, but I've heard he's dating the same gal from last summer."

"The blonde?"

"Seems so." Blair smiled and hugged Stella quickly. Angie observed their profiles, both slim and tall. They were very open to each other, their marriage the stuff of dreams.

"I gotta go, baby. Dad's out of town and someone needs to keep the ship afloat." Blair kissed Stella full on the lips.

"See you at dinner, as long as we don't have too many walk-ins." Stella kissed him back.

In Stella's office, *walk-in* referred to anything from a split lip to lost teeth.

"Do you get a lot of walk-ins this time of year?" Angie asked.

"Hockey pucks." Stella smiled and pointed at her front teeth.

Angie winced. "Ouch. I think I'll stick to analyzing weather patterns."

Stella laughed, then immediately grew solemn.

"Don't worry, Angie. We're all here for you." She looked at her watch. "I've got to go, too. Let's try to get together soon, okay? And no more nonsense about who got pregnant first!"

Angie laughed. "Deal."

CHAPTER FOUR

Present Day
Buffalo, New York

ANGIE LOWERED the car window and let the crisp air wash over her face. For the first time since she'd returned home, she was grateful for the cold. It took her mind off her heaving stomach.

Off her life.

She turned into the parking lot of Koffee Klache. Mom said she'd come over right around two, after she'd checked in on Grandma Violet.

Angie looked at the car's digital clock. One forty-five. She had fifteen minutes to pretend she wasn't pregnant, that her life hadn't taken such a major detour.

Her stomach felt otherwise. She shoved open the door and threw up on Koffee Klache's slush-covered blacktop. When she was done, she leaned back in the seat and tried to will her nausea away. She wouldn't be able to have a coffee, much as she might wish she could. But she didn't want to meet Mom at home. This was more neutral territory.

After several minutes she hauled herself out of the car and into the coffee shop.

"Hi, Angie! The usual?" Molly the barista smiled her welcoming grin. Angie managed to smile back, despite the acrid taste still in her mouth.

"Hey, Molly. Uh, no, not the usual. I'll have an iced ginger tea, please, with some honey."

"You got it." Molly didn't question Angie's choice of "iced," even though it was freezing outside.

The tinkle of the bell above the entrance was followed by the scent of her mother's perfume, which made Angie's stomach roil yet again.

Maybe she should've waited until tonight to meet with her mom. Evenings seemed to be her best time as of late.

"Hi, honey!"

Angie turned around and practically fell into her mother's warm hug. The fuzzy yarn of her mom's scarf tickled Angie's cheeks. She gave Debra a hug back and hoped to pull away as quickly as possible.

But the touch of her mother, the softness of the scarf, even the scent of Debra's perfume, undermined Angie's resolve. For an instant she clung to her mother as though she were six and had just found out she wasn't invited to her friend's birthday party.

"Ange?"

Debra hugged Angie tighter, then drew back and studied her daughter. Angie couldn't believe her mother was nearing sixty. She looked as she'd always looked— better, in fact.

"What do you want to drink, Mom?"

Angie slipped out of her mother's arms and grabbed her own drink from the counter. Debra took the hint and walked over to order.

Angie sat in their usual spot—the two easy chairs by the back window. Her mind echoed with the conversations she and her mother had shared in this space over the years. While Angie was still in high school, the breaks during college and her frequent trips back since settling in San Francisco with Jesse.

No guarantee that Jesse would agree with her decision to stay here, once he found out she was pregnant. When the Director of Operations job opened up at the NOAA facility in Western New York, he'd finally agreed to make a temporary move with her to Buffalo; with his credentials they were both confident that he'd find an equally good—temporary—career opportunity as a neurosurgeon. They'd put their condo up for rent just as Jesse was sent to Iraq.

Part of her felt childish for not telling Jesse the minute she knew she was pregnant. But she wasn't a child anymore; she was a thirty-five-year-old woman about to have her own child.

Debra carried her usual green tea and a small plate of oatmeal raisin cookies to the table. How her mother stayed so slim was beyond Angie. Angie took after her father's side—just one glance at a sweet put the pounds on.

"How's Grandma Vi doing?"

"She's fine." Debra sighed. "I checked on her after knitting group and fixed her an omelet." Angie knew that taking care of Grandma Vi was more complicated now. Something as simple as getting her to eat regularly made a huge difference, but the responsibility tended to take over her mother's life.

Debra's silence confirmed Angie's thoughts.

"How was the group?"

"Fine, fine." Debra busied her hands with settling her coat and her purse; she rested her knitting on her lap. Knitting or anything fiber-related could always lift her mother's spirits.

"What are you making now?" Angie stared at the ball of pink fuzz in Debra's lap. She hoped it wasn't something for her.

Debra laughed. "It looks alive, doesn't it? It's a new yarn. I thought it'd be perfect for your future niece or nephew."

Of course. It was for Blair and Stella's baby.

Angie tried to focus on how great Blair and Stella had been this morning. They weren't pregnant yet, but Angie had no doubt they would be soon. In the most perfect manner, and everyone would know about it.

Blair's twin, Brian, wasn't married yet. But his growing relationship with "the blonde" Blair had mentioned was promising.

And then there was Angie.

Angie glanced up from the yarn into her mother's green eyes. Mom's red hair still corkscrewed around her face, the longer locks a halo about her head. Debra wore an expression reserved for her tough-love moments.

Angie gave a mental groan.

"Are you planning to tell me what's going on or do I have to extract it out of you over this entire pot of tea?"

Angie squirmed at her mother's tone, and the immediate flush of anger at her own childishness annoyed her.

"I'm pregnant."

How's that for an adult statement?

Debra's mouth dropped open and the sound of her ceramic mug hitting the marble mosaic table reverberated.

"You're not!"

"I am, Mom, and I'd appreciate it if you wouldn't even start."

Angie watched as the struggle between tears and joy played across Debra's face. If Angie wasn't so afraid it would make her throw up again, she would have laughed.

"I don't believe it, Mom. You're actually speechless."

"This is wonderful—but you said you never wanted chil—"

"Mom, I said don't start. I mean it."

"What do you expect, Angie? My only daughter tells me she's having my grandchild and I'm supposed to—what? Be quiet?" Debra picked up her tea and gulped down a huge swig.

"Ouch!" She grimaced as she burned her tongue.

"Are you okay, Mom?"

"I'm fine." Debra took a deep breath. She turned her head to the side, her gaze aimed at the huge picture window that looked onto the entrance of the café. But Angie knew Debra wasn't seeing anything but her own thoughts.

Debra turned her face back toward Angie and smiled. "Oh, honey. I've always dreamed of this. I mean, your brother and Stella, they're trying and that's wonderful, but there's something so special about your own daughter having a baby." Debra eyed Angie over her mug. She wasn't done.

"You have other things to consider, sweetheart. You *are* older." Debra reached over and Angie welcomed the warmth of her mother's hand clasping hers.

"Mom, I'm older than you were when you had us, but I'm not ancient, for heaven's sake."

"What does Jesse think?"

Angie looked at her mother.

Debra looked back at her, face expectant. Until realization clouded in her eyes and pursed her lips.

"You *have* told him?"

"Uh, no, not yet. Ughh."

Angie gripped the arms of her chair and inhaled deeply. Her stomach was doing the tango again. Apparently the ginger tea wasn't working its charm.

"No, I haven't told him. What's the point in worrying him when he's so far away? I don't want him to worry about *anything* while he's in such a hotspot."

"Honey, don't you think Jesse would be thrilled to know? That it might give him the extra strength he needs when he's dealing with some of his tougher cases?"

"I haven't even told him I've permanently relocated to Buffalo."

"You *what?*" Debra's eyebrows rose so high on her forehead that Angie wondered if they would completely disappear under her copper bangs.

"I didn't tell him I've moved out here." Angie stared at her glass of tea. It kept the heat flaring out of Debra's eyes from blistering her skin.

"Why not?"

"Lots of reasons. Last year, after I did my dissertation, this opportunity came up. Jesse didn't want to talk about relocating anywhere until he finished his mission. But I couldn't turn down the opportunity to work in Buffalo. He thinks I'm out here for a trial run."

She'd grown tired of her job as resident meteorologist at a local TV station in the Bay Area and had promised herself she'd find something more challenging once she completed her Ph.D. She'd never had to be on television, thank God, but she needed more challenge than the job offered—fairly superficial behind-the-scenes analysis of weather patterns.

That meant she'd had to leave California and life as she and Jesse had known it. Jesse thought it was all temporary, that they'd go back to California if the "experimental" career changes didn't work for either one of them. But she'd decided on her own to make her position permanent.

She didn't want to think about the dangers Jesse faced today and every day since he'd left. He was a top neurosurgeon and when the chance had arisen to help save lives in Iraq, he took it with no hesitation.

"That's why you've been so dodgy whenever I asked how long your contract is with NOAA." Debra knew Angie had landed a coveted position with the National Oceanic and Atmospheric Administration in Buffalo.

"I'm here to stay, Mom. I want the baby to know my family, to have cousins. In San Francisco I'd be on my own."

And reminded too much of what she might lose with Jesse. She didn't want him to think she'd "tricked" him into the pregnancy. They'd both had a good time that night and she'd had no indication that she was fertile. Up until now, their protective measures had worked....

"You know your father and I support you, honey."

"Mom, don't go blaming yourself for this. This has nothing to do with you or Dad or our color."

Angie was well aware that her mom often wondered if their children suffered because of their interracial background. Debra was from a Polish-American family in one of Buffalo's poorer suburbs.

Dad was from an educated African-American family and had grown up in an affluent neighborhood. Debra had been her family's first to go to college and to have a real career. Will was just another son in a long line of college-graduate professionals.

Angie considered herself both black and white, although she knew many people saw her as African-American, especially in areas that were still predominately white. She'd been born with her dad's curly hair and the lighter brown skin of her paternal grandmother. She had Debra's green eyes.

On the West Coast, in the anonymity and cultural diversity of San Francisco, she'd never felt her skin color was an issue. She'd been free to become the woman she was today.

"You know, I have a better idea of what you're going through than you realize."

"*Really*, Mom?" Angie tried to keep her tone neutral, but if she had a cookie for every time Mom said she "knew" what Angie was feeling, Angie would weigh three hundred pounds.

"Seriously, Angie. I was younger, it was a different era, but I expected to raise you on my own."

"You were married, though."

"Well, after I was pregnant with you. As a matter of fact, it was after I'd *had* you."

"*After* I was born?"

Debra steadied her gaze on Angie. "Your dad and I were almost—" she shook her head "—no, we *were* high-school sweethearts. Or at least we were meant to be."

Heat rushed into Angie's face as she stared at her mother. "Why don't I already know this?"

Debra flicked her fingers against her mug. "No reason to bring it up before. Do you really want to know the details?"

Angie didn't hesitate. "Yes. And start with the high-school stuff."

CHAPTER FIVE

February 1967
Buffalo, New York

"YOU HAVE A LOT of homework this weekend?"

Will looked at Debra with what she thought were the most beautiful brown eyes on earth.

"Not too much." She felt suddenly shy as they stood on the sidewalk where the school bus had dropped them off minutes ago. Cars whizzed past on the busy street Kenmore Avenue had become as they'd grown up.

"Trigonometry going okay?" Will always asked how she was doing. Deb was taking all advanced courses, so although she was only a sophomore she was well on her way to college-level credits by her junior and senior years.

Just like Will.

"Yeah. I did have a bit of trouble with this one problem, but I'll get it."

"Why don't I help you?"

Deb smiled at Will and nodded. "That'd be great." Truth was, she didn't need any help. From the beginning, school had been her escape and now promised to be her ticket out of the Buffalo neighborhood her entire family seemed to live in. College would be her passport to a better life.

"Let's go over to my house and I'll get my notes from two years ago. Then we can work in Dad's office."

"Great." Although going to his house made her nervous, she fell into step beside Will, marveling, as she often did, at how well they spent time together. They were both excellent students and enjoyed a lot of the same literature.

But she'd become aware of a tension between them over the past year or so. Nothing bad, just…different. She knew what it was; she'd had crushes on boys before. But they'd always faded.

And Will always remained her best friend.

"I'll wait for you in the office while you get your notebook, okay?" This was their usual routine. Deb waited in Dr. Bradley's office, while Will got what he needed from his house.

Debra didn't go over to Will's anymore. They'd stopped hanging out in his house a few years back, when Will started high school. His mom wasn't keen on it. Said their age difference was too great.

Deb's mom didn't really know how many afternoons Deb spent studying with Will. Deb would never dare bring Will home. It was an unspoken rule that Deb's mom and extended family wouldn't go for her bringing a black boy to the house, even as a friend.

Deb told her mother as little as possible. She still worked for Will's dad in the doctor's office and didn't raise an eyebrow whenever Deb and Will came in and did homework there the way they used to as kids. The office was neutral territory. Most days, though, they went to the public library.

"I'd like it if you came with me to the house, Deb." Will had a strange look on his face. Deb wondered if something had happened at school that Will needed to talk about.

"Well, okay, I guess." She trudged through the slush alongside him. The heavy snowfall from last week had melted into this mess, but would freeze up again by nightfall.

"Thanks." Will loped comfortably next to her, but she still sensed an uneasiness in him.

"Is everything okay, Will?"

"Yeah, yeah, everything's great. And don't worry about Mama, she's at her charity work today."

Relief washed over Debra. So Will's house was empty, unless their housekeeper was still there. Mrs. Bradley was nothing but polite to her. But Angie understood she was *persona non grata* in Violet's opinion. White and poor. Not a match for Will.

As they got to the house, the wind picked up.

"The storm's coming in quick." Deb lifted her face to the breeze that was getting colder by the minute.

"You've loved storms since we were kids." Will stared at her and she gazed back at him.

"Yes, I suppose I have. You noticed that?"

"I notice more than you ever realize, Deb."

Will's handsome face looked so good to Deb. But she noticed the twitch along his jawline.

He kept staring at her as though he'd never seen her before.

"What is it, Will?"

He swallowed visibly and drew in a deep breath.

"Deb, you know I'm going to Howard University in the fall."

The pain that pinched her stomach frightened her.

"Yes, I know that. But it's only February."

"My senior year. You'll be in college in two more years yourself, Deb."

"Yes, yes, I will." And she couldn't wait!

"Maybe Ivy League."

"Maybe." She'd worked so hard on her studies, in the hopes of a full scholarship.

"My point is that we'll be far away from each other after this year."

"Will, we'll still be friends!"

"I don't want to be just your friend, Deb."

"Oh." It was her turn to swallow. Her insides trembled and it wasn't from the cold or wind.

"Deb. You mean the world to me."

Will pulled off his backpack and dropped it on the concrete porch. He stepped closer to Deb, leaving barely an inch between them.

"I can't imagine my life without you." He placed his hands on either side of her face. Debra thrilled to the electric shivers his touch sent across her skin.

"I know." She couldn't say anymore, daren't. She didn't want tears to mess this up.

"Deb. May I?"

"Yes."

He lowered his head and she watched it all. Will's dark, smooth skin. His eyelids lowering, his breath making a cloud between them. His lips touched hers and Debra closed her eyes.

It was better than Debra had ever allowed herself to imagine. Will was sweet, tender and very much a gentleman. After the first contact he continued to kiss her, over and over.

Debra had never experienced anything so delicious in her entire life.

"Will!"

Will and Debra jerked apart at the shrill sound of his mother's voice.

Debra looked over her shoulder and saw Mrs. Bradley standing in the entry behind the storm door. They hadn't heard it open.

But Violet Bradley had heard *them*. Apparently her charity work wasn't today, after all.

Will recovered first.

"Hi, Mom." He leaned down and grabbed his backpack.

Deb stood there, shaking. Her most exciting moment had quickly soured. Violet Bradley hated her. Tears of humiliation and pride pricked at Debra's eyelids.

"Get in here, son!"

"Yes, Mom." Will shrugged, turning to Debra.

"I'll meet you in the office in a few minutes."

"Okay." Debra nodded at Mrs. Bradley. She didn't wait for an acknowledgment. The look on Violet's face told Debra that Will was in for a battle.

Debra all but ran down the steps and back through the woods to the office. After saying a quick hello to her own mother at the receptionist's desk, she sat down in the back inventory room where she and Will usually did their homework.

Debra pulled her trigonometry out of her backpack and opened her binder to her notes. She settled into her English assignment, *The Tempest,* while she waited.

Will never came.

CHAPTER SIX

Present Day
Buffalo, New York
Debra

IT WASN'T EASY to keep from bursting into torrents of laughter at the shocked look on Angie's face.

What, did she think her parents never had sex? Poor thing, with her morning sickness and all.

My sense of humor wasn't always in tune with everyone else's, and I was sure Angie found nothing funny about what I told her.

I kept my cool as I drove. I needed to get to the welcome nest of our home. Mine and Will's.

I pulled into our long, wooded driveway and parked in front of the house. I'd teased Will mercilessly that he should just have built a tree house. It was what our place reminded me of.

It was built only twenty years ago, Will's design, but looked as though it has been part of these woods forever. The cedar siding and A-frame structure blended perfectly with the trees.

The house cost us a fortune at the time. Will wanted to design the home we'd live in for the rest of our lives, and he wouldn't settle for less.

I was glad he didn't.

We came here when the kids were still young, Angie fourteen and the twins in grade school. I had so many joyous memories of raising those kids in this home.

Angie.

My daughter can be impetuous, and this latest stunt was no exception.

A baby! Without her husband....

I was going to be a grandmother. But not how I'd expected.

Since Blair and Stella had been trying to get pregnant, I hadn't considered any other possibilities. Certainly not Angie....

The fact that she hadn't told Jesse bothered me. He was working in the middle of a war zone, under stress, but to know he was going to be a father would boost his morale, wouldn't it?

They'd been married for seven years. Angie didn't discuss it, but I'd always thought they'd have kids at some point, when it was important enough to both of them.

I went inside and threw my knitting bag on the old cane chair from Will's father's old office.

The office where I met Will, all those years ago.

I looked around for our dog.

"Rose!"

The golden retriever was up in my room, no doubt, her ears pricked to my arrival but not wanting to leave her warm bed. Will loved that dog so much. Rose was spoiled more than the kids had ever been.

"C'mon, Rose! We've got to check on Vi."

Rose came out and padded down the stairs. Her tail

wagged at the mention of Vi. That dog was crazy about Vi, something that stumped me, as Vi was never very affectionate to her.

"Let's go."

We walked out the back kitchen door and I left Rose outside in the yard as I knocked, then entered Vi's cottage. She never locked the door.

"Vi?" The kitchen light over the sink was on. I saw the back of Vi's silver head on the other side of her cream sofa.

"Oh, hey." She raised a thin hand as I circled the room and gave her a careful look.

"How are you doing? Did the meds help?"

"Yes. I'm sorry I bothered you when you were out having fun with the girls. How was your coffee with Angie?" Vi always made it sound as though my life was one big party.

"You didn't bother me. Angie sends her love. How about some tea? Have you eaten lunch?" Judging by the lack of dishes in her sink, Vi hadn't moved from the couch since I'd checked in on her before I went to the Koffee Klache.

"Yes, I made myself a sandwich."

"Are you sure?" I nosed around the kitchen a bit. No sign of even a crumb. Ahh, there was the evidence—a butter knife with a mustard smear.

"Yes, I'm fine—resting now."

I turned on the water and washed the knife for her. The cottage had a dishwasher but Vi wouldn't use it—said it was "too much" for just her.

I made us both tea and took the cups into the sitting room.

"You can put your show back on, Vi."

"No, no, that's okay." *Liar.* I knew she watched her soaps every day, and she knew I knew. I grabbed the remote and clicked on the television.

"Here, have some tea."

"Thanks." Vi was quiet as she sipped the tea and watched her program.

I sighed inwardly. I had so much to get ready for the art show, including the weaving that needed to be finished. But I couldn't ask Vi to come over and stay at our place if I was only going to disappear into my studio.

And she needed company, whether she asked for it or not.

I needed to be in Will's arms. Three days until he was back from Los Angeles. I'd have a pot roast on the table. And our king-size bed would be waiting for him....

How lucky was I that I still had a great sex life with the same man who'd taught me how to make love in Paris, almost forty years ago?

September 1972
Paris, France

THE THREE-HUNDRED-YEAR-OLD building triggered countless visions in Will's mind. He saw the building architecturally—the ribs exposed, before the marble and plaster added their depth. His mind's eye pictured each layer, one after another, until the interior looked as it did today.

The sound of his leather soles on the wide stairway comforted him. Will lived and breathed architecture.

He walked down the ornate hallway to a familiar

classroom. Once a ballroom, it had been converted with utilitarian chairs and desks. The first architectural design class he'd taken this summer had been in this room. The days were long, sweaty and intellectually exhilarating.

Today was the start of his art in architecture class. He hoped the professor was more of a left-brain type so they'd study building structure more than actual artwork like paintings and sculpture. Either way, this was a required class for his graduate studies abroad, so he'd do whatever he had to do.

He wasn't really into the Paris art scene; he had his sights set on becoming America's foremost architect.

He slid into a seat toward the back. He was early and only two other students had shown up so far. He opened a notebook and flipped through it. He'd loved his class this summer, and his French had improved with each passing week. This class had the potential to be great, as well.

Or boring as hell.

As he perused his notebook, an unopened envelope fell out.

From Sarah.

He sighed. Hell-bent as he was on becoming a great architect, his mother and Sarah were equally hell-bent on his marrying Sarah.

Both from Western New York, they'd met on campus at Howard University. Sarah had moved back to Buffalo from Washington, D.C., after graduation. She worked as a legal researcher in downtown Buffalo.

The one time he'd taken her out, over spring break, she'd made it clear that she'd follow Will anywhere, even if it was "back here to little ol' Buffalo."

She'd had the same privileged upbringing he had. Money had buffered them from some of the effects of racism his poorer black friends had suffered.

They were a great match on paper. But he didn't love Sarah. Not the way he thought he should.

Hell, what did he know?

He'd had his nose in books for the past five years. And he suspected that his mother was determined to win the marriage war, since his parents had lost their battle to send him to med school.

Long legs in fishnet stockings caught his eye.

A woman with a short plaid skirt and black knee-high boots moved quickly to the seat in front of him. Her figure was accentuated by her red mohair sweater, over which fell a riot of bright carrot-colored curls. His fingers knew how her curls would feel, how they'd spring back from his tug.

He'd known a woman with hair like this once. A girl. But she was in Buffalo, part of his past, and he'd never see her again.

Couldn't.

The scent of the woman's perfume made his blood run hot. So much so that he didn't realize the professor had arrived and started taking attendance.

"Roman?"

"*Ici.*"

"Russert?"

"*Ici.*"

"Schaefer?"

"*Oui, ici, madame.*"

That voice.

"Debra?" he whispered, afraid he'd lost his mind.

The woman with the cloud of red hair turned around in her seat. Her green eyes glittered in the morning light shafting through the Murano glass windowpanes. The same freckles, the same tilt of her nose. But on a much more sophisticated face. Was that glossy lipstick on her naturally pink lips?

She didn't recognize him for a heartbeat, but then recognition and incredulity lit up her expression.

"Will!" Her voice was huskier, sexier than he'd remembered.

And too loud for Professor Cleremont.

"This is a graduate-level course and very demanding, Mademoiselle Schaefer."

Debra whirled back around in her chair.

"Oui, Madame Cleremont." Her French was flawless. Will recalled that she'd taken French in high school, but when had she learned to speak like a native?

He sat behind her for the next hour and forty-five minutes, not hearing a single word of what Professor Cleremont said. His intense and constant awareness of Debra made him feel flushed. Distracted.

So his reaction to their one shared kiss at seventeen—when she was fifteen—hadn't been a fluke. At least not for him.

The class finally ended and Will absently picked up the handouts as the fifteen students filed out the door. He saw only one.

Debra.

"When did you get here?" Without thought, he

placed his hand on her elbow. She stopped and turned to face him. He had her full attention, all right.

"Last week. This is my junior year abroad with Mount Holyoke."

"Mount Holyoke?"

She looked exasperated.

"Yes, Will. I'm a student. I attend university. I'm studying art history."

"But Mount Holyoke's Ivy League."

Her eyes narrowed.

"There is such a thing as a scholarship, Will."

"But…you're still an undergrad—these are graduate courses."

"Yes, and I'm earning my master's at the same time as my bachelor's." Her face reflected boredom and a flash of…disappointment?

"I never knew—"

"You never bothered to ask, Will."

Ouch. He hadn't contacted her after their kiss that winter day so long ago. His mother had forbidden any contact with her, and frankly he didn't want his mother on Debra's case, either.

He'd felt the need to protect her, although—or perhaps because—they moved in different circles. The same high school but vastly different social groups. He couldn't remember Debra ever being at a dance or after-school function. He'd missed her terribly but was more relieved than anything. He didn't want his friends bothering her.

They'd never spoken again.

"Yeah. I guess we…drifted apart."

"Call it whatever you want, Will. I have another class in half an hour, across the *place.*"

With that she stalked away from him and he just stood there, his breath gone. As though she'd punched him in the stomach, hard. But she hadn't even touched him.

She'd given him that look—of contempt? Disapproval?—with her brilliant eyes. The eyes that used to radiate hero worship for him.

The eyes that glowed softly in the winter moonlight after he'd kissed her, his hands on either side of her face. He hadn't felt the cold blustering around them.

Just the wonder of childhood companionship that had grown into something deeper.

And was cut off.

Will shivered in the autumn sunshine.

A moment earlier, her eyes had done the same thing to him. She'd cut him off.

September 1972
Paris, France

DEBRA HAD NO IDEA how she did it. She'd walked away from Will after missing him for all these years. His memory had spoiled the chances of every boyfriend since.

She liked boys. A lot, in fact.

But when it came to talking about things that mattered, they were dumb asses compared to Will. How could they be anything else? She and Will had shared a childhood friendship that could never be recaptured with anyone else.

It didn't mean she couldn't find the same level of intimacy with anyone else, did it?

So far she hadn't. But she was still young.

She snorted and heaved her book bag higher on her shoulder.

Pretty pathetic that she compared college men to a boy she'd known in Buffalo.

Buffalo.

Ha! Will's expression had said it all. He'd never expected her to amount to anything, much less run into her here, of all places. Although a small, hidden part of her was saddened by that, part of her was exuberant.

She'd far exceeded everyone's expectations, even her own.

One of her favorite things about Paris beckoned, and she stopped at a café, ordering coffee and a croissant. The waiter sent her an appreciative glance.

Debra gave him the smile she'd perfected over the summer. It was her "thanks for the thought but no chance, pal" smile. His own smile faded and he turned away.

She sipped her coffee and gazed at the people strolling by her table. Since it wasn't raining, she sat outside to soak up the sun, reveling in the sparkling fountain across the street.

She was far away from the days of survival in Buffalo, living with mom in their one-bedroom duplex.

Poor Mom. She'd done the best she could. Eventually she'd met a man who was able to offer her companionship as well as help her out financially. They lived out in Crabapple Lake, a suburb Debra hadn't even heard of when she was a kid. She thought life began and ended in her city neighborhood.

With Will.

She looked at the potted flowers on the café's terrace. The yellow blooms seemed to be stretching for their last moments of sunlight before winter set in.

She liked the weather here, much milder than Boston, certainly more so than Buffalo.

Will hadn't realized how smart she was. She hadn't, either, until her SAT scores came back and she'd found out she could go to just about any college she wanted. Harvard was an obvious choice but she'd settled on Mount Holyoke. It seemed more intimate, and the all-girl environment enticed her. She'd hoped to find the sister she'd never had. A girlfriend who wasn't intimidated by her intelligence.

Amy had stepped into that void in her life. The girl from Iowa had shared her sense of adventure and wide-eyed wonder at their good fortune in freshman year. They'd both left impoverished situations, ending up in the Mecca of American education.

And elitism.

Elitism wasn't new to Debra.

She'd met Will's mother.

"What are you doing here? Don't you have a class?" The question ripped her out of her musings.

Amy, also her Parisian flatmate, stood in front of the table, blocking the sunlight.

"No, not until two." She'd lied to Will. Why did that bother her?

"Great. Want to go check out the library?"

"Which one?"

She dropped the appropriate coins on the table and grabbed her backpack. A walk through yet another beautiful building was distinctly preferable to her Buffalo memories.

CHAPTER SEVEN

October 1972
Paris, France

"DEBRA?" Amy called.

Amy walked back into the small flat's parlor with the person who'd rung their doorbell.

"Will!"

His presence drew every ounce of her attention.

How had he found her? More important, why?

"I have a class a block away in a couple of hours, and I wondered if you'd like to get a cup of coffee with me?"

Amy's polite cough distracted Debra. Only then did she see her friend's curious expression.

"Sorry. Amy, this is Will, Will, my flatmate, Amy." At Amy's arched eyebrow, Debra added, "Will's an old friend from my hometown. We've known each other since we were kids."

"Nice to meet you, Will."

"A pleasure."

Will grasped Amy's hand. Debra was horrified yet intrigued at the stab of jealousy that streaked across her awareness.

Will turned back to her.

"Ready?"

"Let me get my coat." The temperature had started to drop, and the nights required a jacket or heavy sweater.

"Great." His expression was so relaxed, as though he and Debra did this all the time. As though he took girls out all the time.

Stupid jealousy.

Debra ignored Amy's stifled giggles and unspoken questions.

"Later," she muttered to her flatmate as she and Will left.

Debra was grateful for the sting of the cold night air that hit her cheeks as soon as they were outside.

In silent agreement they headed toward the river.

"So, how have your classes been going?" Will's expression was one of total concentration on her. Debra had missed their bond more than she'd admitted to herself.

"Great. I still can't believe I'm here. I've always dreamed of studying in Paris, and, well, here I am." She sounded so dumb, so suburban!

She bit her lip to keep from saying anything else inane.

"I know what you mean. It's unreal, isn't it? Paris is so far from Buffalo."

His stride was much longer than hers, but he fell into step next to her. She didn't feel rushed or anxious. It had always been easy between her and Will.

She noticed another mixed-race couple passing near them.

"Yes, it sure is far from home." Her voice had a hitch in it she couldn't control.

"Do you go back often?"

They waited to cross the street, and she turned to look at him. He smiled at her. The light in his eyes and the shape of his lips were so familiar to her. Yet different.

This was a more intense version of the Will she'd known. The Will she thought of as her first love.

An intense longing started deep in her belly and spread out through her limbs. Her reaction caught her off guard.

The light changed and Debra broke their eye contact.

She stepped off the curb and struggled to resume their conversation.

"When I was in Boston I'd go back at Christmas. I used to go home at Thanksgiving, too, if I could find a ride. But it's just too far for such a short visit. And with doubling up on my courses, I can't afford all that time away during the school year."

"I hear you." He smiled at her. "And what have you been doing during the summers?"

"I do co-op work to earn spending money." Her cheeks burned and her ire flared. She had nothing to be ashamed of. "I have a full academic ride," she went on to explain, "but I like to have the funds for all the extras." Why did she need to justify herself to him?

Will smiled at her again and the warmth in his eyes made her oblivious to the stiff wind that whisked up leaves on the street.

"I go back home and work at an architecture firm when I have time. These past two summers I've been in class, though."

They walked in silence. Of course he was in class all the time. His parents were able to afford the best for Will.

"How's your brother?"

"He's doing great, but he's pissed off my folks." He looked at her sideways. "Sorry for the cussing."

"I've heard worse." She didn't say that the worst words she'd heard were from her mother. She didn't have to; Will knew.

"How did your brother upset your parents?" She asked the question knowing it didn't take much to anger Will's mother.

"He went to West Point."

"Really?" she asked in surprise.

"Yeah. He wanted to serve his country, but if he'd enlisted it really would've killed Mom and Dad. This was a better choice, although they're still mad at him."

Debra didn't comment.

His family would've expected Jimmy to attend a historically black college or university, as Will had, and wanted him to pursue a respected civilian profession. The military was never part of the plans they had for their children, she was sure.

Will's family was one of the more distressing memories of Buffalo she preferred to leave buried.

She shuddered and shoved her hands deeper into her coat pockets.

"It's getting chilly at night, isn't it?" she murmured. They were on the right bank of the Seine, walking with dozens, possibly hundreds, of others. Yet it felt as it always had with Will.

As though they were the only two people in the universe.

"Spoken like a true Buffalo gal."

They laughed.

"Yeah, where else is 'chilly' just above freezing?"

"Or a 'nice day' any day with sun and less than a foot of snow?" He laughed again. "I've missed our conversations, Deb."

"Me, too." But she didn't want to explore why they hadn't been able to keep in touch. Because, in the end, it always came back to one thing. The chasm between their backgrounds and families.

Several couples passed. What did they look like to others? Simply students? Good friends? Or more?

"Did you already eat?" Polite as ever. Thinking of her.

"Yes, Amy and I eat earlier than most Parisians."

"And it's cheaper to eat in."

"You got it." Although she doubted Will had to worry about how much any meal cost, even over here. She noticed how he'd matured since she'd last seen him. His facial features were more chiseled, his body more powerful, more purposeful in its movements.

"Do you eat in or usually go out?"

He shrugged his broad shoulders. "I do whatever's easiest. I basically live on baguettes with ham and cheese. Sometimes I treat myself to a hot meal in one of the cafés at lunch, but not too often."

"Have you tried the student mess?" She found it the most reasonable place to get a decent meal.

"Yeah, but it's not practical for me. I only have one class a week near there."

"Have *you* eaten, Will?"

"Actually, no. Would you mind sitting with me while I dine?"

"That sounds so formal."

He paused, and she stopped next to him. The wind whipped at their faces and her eyes smarted.

"I don't mean to sound formal. I just think it's incredible that we've run into each other again, Deb, and I'm at a loss for what to say to you. My family was so unbelievably rude—"

"Stop." She placed her gloved hands on his arm. "That's so far in the past, Will. I don't want to talk about it. We're in Paris, for heaven's sake! People are more open-minded here."

His eyes reflected the glint of the streetlamps off the water.

"Deb, you were my best friend growing up. I'm still angry at myself for allowing my mo—"

She held up her hand. "No, I mean it, Will. If we're going to be friends here, I don't want to talk about it. Deal?"

She lowered her hand and offered it to him.

He grasped her fingers and even through her wool gloves she felt the charge of awareness course between them.

"Deal."

He held on to her hand a beat longer than necessary. Debra tugged it free. She'd have to be very careful or she'd end up believing she and Will were *more* than childhood friends.

"Where did you have in mind for dinner?"

"I have a favorite place near Saint Chapelle. It's small, loud and cheap. Oh, and the food's great." His teeth flashed in the evening light.

"Lead the way."

CHAPTER EIGHT

Present Day
Buffalo, New York
Debra

"YOU SOUND AS THOUGH you aren't surprised." I had the phone tucked to my shoulder as I folded laundry. We'd already discussed Vi's health and were on to the children. The day had dawned bright, and sunlight danced on the snow-covered ground.

"They're young and in love. We've been there, haven't we, baby?" Will's baritone tickled my ear even over the phone, thirty-five-hundred miles away.

I sighed.

"Yes, but our circumstances were quite different."

"Honey, I know you're worried about Angie. But I have a feeling this will all work out. Yes, our circumstances were different. To many folks they still are."

"What about to you, Will?"

"You know me, Deb. I don't give a flying—"

"I know you don't care what others think." I cut him off before he blistered my ear. "But I want you to tell me what *you* think. Has it been worth it?"

"Worth it? You mean you're not sure?"

"I am as far as you and I are concerned. But the kids, Will, are they still paying the price?"

"They had every comfort growing up, including the best education possible. It wasn't easy for them being mixed, but life's hard, sweetheart. And they had it a hell of a lot easier than we ever did."

I'd angered him. Will was so defensive about the decision we made to share our lives. To raise the kids with all the love and support we'd both missed in our own childhoods. Never mind the issue of mixed race. Will prided himself on having taken the best lessons from his own childhood to use as a measure of how he'd been as a father to our children. He always took it personally when I mentioned my concerns about the kids and their childhood.

"Yes and no, Will."

"What are you wearing?" He'd lowered his voice and I smiled into the receiver.

"Nothing. I'm folding laundry in front of the kitchen windows, buck-naked." I looked down at the fuzzy sweats and slippers I wore.

"Mmm, I want you to fold *me* up."

I couldn't help laughing.

"Day after tomorrow, Will. And we're not done with this conversation."

"I didn't expect we were."

Again I laughed. Will knew me best. I had to talk everything out to the last detail. He was more of an internal-operations type when it came to emotions.

"Still arriving at the same time?"

"Yeah, the red-eye. But maybe you'll take a nap with me when I get in?" Will hated flying at night. He treasured his own bed, and having me to snuggle up with.

"I'm working out of the home studio all day tomorrow."

"See you then, babe. Love you."

"Love you, too."

After we hung up I finished folding the laundry and headed upstairs to get dressed for the day. For the moment I put my frustration on hold—Will always tried to distract me with sex when he didn't want to deal with the conflicts between us.

I carried the laundry basket upstairs with me and left it on the bed. I would put away the clean clothes later.

I yanked the yellowed doily my grandmother had crocheted over sixty years ago off the top of the long cedar chest at the foot of our bed. Cedar chests were one of my indulgences over the years. They were the best kind of storage for my artwork and items of knitted clothing I couldn't bear to part with after long hours of knitting, ripping out, reknitting.

The aroma of cedar, wool and baby rose from the chest when I opened the lid. It was as if the old chests breathed. In a sense, they did. They were alive with memories.

Knitting had been my refuge through most of my life.

I couldn't remember what I was wearing or how my hair looked on any given day. But I did remember exactly where I was when I knit each sweater, each pair of socks or mittens, and of course, all my wall hangings. Just the feeling of a project took me back to that particular time.

So many different wools and other fibers brushed my fingers as I dug through the chest, but I ignored them. I was on a mission. I wanted to find the baby items I'd knitted for Angie.

When was the last time I'd been in this chest?

I hadn't even looked in here when Blair and Stella got married, or when they started talking about babies. The twins' items were all in a different chest, in the guest room that they shared as boys.

My fingers rubbed against the soft fuzzy yarn I knew was Angie's layette.

Eager to remember how small she'd been and how my stitches had formed these tiny outfits, I pulled on the bundle of cloth, mindless of the layers I disturbed.

I smiled in anticipation of my long-ago treasure.

I was wrong. In my hands I held some of Angie's baby clothes, but my gaze didn't rest on the pink-and-white cardigans. I stared at the bright red scarf that had been knit by my five-year-old hands.

Sorrow reached up from the depths of the chest and grabbed me, shaking me hard.

This wasn't some memory I'd shoved down or needed hours of therapy to resolve.

It was what I'd known all my life.

My dad left us when I was five. The last day I saw him, he'd packed his suitcases as he always did before a trip and gave me the usual hug.

"Can you bring me something back, Daddy?"

"Sure, sweetheart. What do you want?"

"A teddy bear. Brown."

"You bet, Debbie girl."

He'd tousled my hair and was gone. I didn't know I'd never see him again, ever. I believed he'd come back, and that he'd bring me my teddy bear. I knitted the scarf for that damned bear, and here it was, fifty-three years later, still alone.

My mother was right, in her coarse, matter-of-fact way.

"That sonofabitch didn't have the decency to tell us to our faces that he was going for good. Didn't make sure we were taken care of."

It was a verse ingrained in my life, as I'd heard my mother sing my father's curses until well after she'd met her current husband, Fred. But I was a little girl and he'd been my prince.

I fingered the tiny red scarf. If not for my first prince abandoning me, I'd never have met the real prince of my life.

Will.

"SOY NO-WHIP MOCHA, right?" Phil O'Leary placed the brand-name coffee cup on Angie's desk.

"Thanks, Phil." She looked up at him from the bank of screens that displayed various measures of Buffalo's meteorological status. As the new Director of Operations, Angie knew her staff watched her closely, and she needed to be as informed as they were on the weather.

"My pleasure." Angie noted that, indeed, Phil seemed quite pleased with himself. Her assistant had fallen all over himself to impress her since she'd arrived four weeks ago.

At some point she was going to have to tell him she

wasn't interested, but she didn't want to seem uncaring or unappreciative. One thing she remembered about this city—it was a friendly place.

Unlike the West Coast where she'd lived during her post-graduate years and early career, people in Buffalo treated everyone like family. There wasn't much of a "getting-to-know-you" phase.

The weather grid was typical for a northern New York February—including the possibility of a severe winter storm by the end of the week. Angie loved the thrill of watching the huge system take shape. The weather in San Francisco had its moments, but not the unpredictability of a Buffalo winter.

"I hope you've bought some cold-weather gear since you transferred." Phil chuckled and shook his head at the monitors. "It's going to get dicey over the next few days."

Phil loved talking. Angie did, too, but not at work. And definitely not when she was putting her own forecast together.

"Phil, have you found out any more about the interns from the university? Do we have enough room for them over spring break? And what about the grad students who've requested interviews?"

Phil took the hint and went to his desk, still wearing his benign smile.

Angie's own smile left her face as soon as she turned back to the screens and morning reports. The watch-floor meeting was in fifteen minutes.

The weather team would have their analysis ready, but she liked to form her own opinion first. That way there was less chance of missing an important detail or being off on the timing.

The storm analysis wasn't holding her attention like it usually did. The mess she'd made of her life was distracting her.

The baby proclaimed his or her presence more every day. Her breasts and belly were visibly swollen and her face was fuller, flushed with the new life inside.

She needed to tell Jesse. Mom was right about that. But she didn't want him to think she'd planned this behind his back or wasn't listening to his opinions and wishes.

Neither of them had wanted children for the longest time, but she'd been feeling the urge to have a baby over the past two years. She'd mentioned it to Jesse, and while he didn't say they'd *never* have kids, he didn't want to plan on it for the near future.

His childhood had been abusive at the hands of alcoholic, drug-addicted parents. Though they were clean and sober now, Jesse didn't want to pass any risk of addiction to his own children. He had a brother and a sister, both of whom had kids who appeared to be healthy and well-adjusted. But Angie had never been able to convince Jesse that he'd make a wonderful parent, too. He said he was content to be the favorite uncle to his nieces and nephews.

Angie swirled the coffee in her cup. She had to tell him, but she felt it should be in person.

At the right moment.

Hopping a flight to Iraq was out of the question, so she might have to compromise on the "in person" part.

Present Day
Buffalo, New York
Debra

THE NEXT MORNING Will came in before I'd had a chance to start work in my studio. My exhibit was ever present in my mind and I had some finishing touches to research. I'd planned a display of my different artwork over the years, with black-and-white photos of historical events as backdrops to each piece.

"Debra?" His voice found me upstairs in the oversize reading chair we kept in the alcove off our master bedroom. After all this time, I still felt a little shiver of delight at the sound of his voice.

My girlfriends and I agreed that business trips help keep the home fires burning. We had friends, couples, who'd slipped into such a predictable pattern that they didn't appreciate each other any longer. The respect died, and its bitter embers fueled resentment and loathing.

"Up here."

I quickly cleared off my lap and shoved the baby book under the chair. Will never took well to my reminiscing. He assumed it meant I was not happy in the present.

Nothing could be further from true. I was just looking for some photos of Angie wearing the outfits I'd finally dug out—after I got over finding Teddy's scarf.

The hallway floorboards creaked under Will's steps. He was a large man, but still lean and graceful on his feet. He'd never been a star athlete but his twice-weekly tennis games with colleagues, combined with our weekend hikes, kept him trim.

And sexy as hell.

"Hey, have you been waiting for me?" The twinkle in his eyes sent a tickle through my belly.

"Always, dear," I answered demurely.

We met each other halfway across the carpeted room. I closed my eyes before his lips touched mine. He gave me his usual I'm-home-dammit-and-I-want-you kiss before enveloping me in his large arms.

I rested my head against his shoulder, accessible due to his half-bent position, inhaling the scent that was Will.

I squeezed him tighter. This was when I felt the best with Will. When we were alone, just us, and none of life's potential ugliness had a chance to intrude.

We'd learned to put differences aside if we wanted to keep our sex life healthy. There'd always be time for talking and rehashing different points of view.

"What have you been doing this morning?" His gaze took in the still-open chest at the foot of the bed, with knitted sweaters, socks, mittens and afghans strewn everywhere.

"I've been going through my treasures, thinking about our future grandkids—and the art exhibit." I fingered a mohair cap. "Just looking for a little inspiration."

"Obviously I've been gone too long." He smiled as he observed that his side of our king-size bed was heaped with skeins of yarn and pattern books.

"Yes, you have. You're going to be a grandparent!" I grinned at his expression. Bemusement mixed with awe, giving him a vulnerable look.

"Yes, I am. We are." He tugged off his tie and went to the walk-in closet. "Did you have anything planned for dinner tonight?"

"Not really. There's some stew I froze last week after we had the kids over. I can heat that up and make a quick salad." When we were younger and Will was gone, I'd often whipped up a gourmet meal for his return. But more recently we both preferred lighter, simpler fare.

"How about I take you out, Grandma?" The laugh that followed his query echoed from the closet.

"How about you let our *grandchild* call me Grandma?"

He laughed again and came back into the bedroom. He'd changed into black jeans and a casual burnt-orange button-down shirt. The color reflected superbly off his still-smooth coffee skin.

"Hey, handsome." I lifted the hem of my knit top. "Wanna play before you take a nap?"

His hands were on the flat of my belly, the curve of my back, his lips on my neck.

"Sure do, sweetheart. Sure do…."

February 1973
Paris, France

"I'VE MISSED YOU."

Debra's skin warmed at Will's statement.

She leaned toward him over the six-inch hedge that separated them as they walked through the public garden. They held hands over the small expanse between them.

"Liar."

"I haven't been able to come by as often because of my project. But it's in the bag now."

"The papers and exams can be overwhelming, can't they?"

She marveled at how perfectly their hands fit together.

The hedgerow ended and Will stopped. They were in one of the most breathtaking gardens in all of Paris, beautiful even in winter, yet Debra saw only Will. It wasn't just his large frame, his heat or his deep voice. It was an aura she couldn't see, but her heart beat faster every time she sensed him near.

"I don't want to talk about school right now, Deb."

She met his gaze, thrilled by the warmth in his eyes. "Okay."

He sighed and glanced around them. "I know this isn't Buffalo, that they're more open here. But I can't bring myself to do anything other than hold hands in public. I don't want anyone to look at you differently."

She loved how he put her first, allowed the decision to be hers. But Debra's impatience to be with him spurred her on. "Will, I don't care what other people think. You know that much about me."

He hadn't forgotten that, had he?

"Deb, *I* care what other people think. I could've ruined your entire reputation, cost you your friends, back in high school."

Her throat tightened around her breath. "They weren't my friends."

All but one of her girlfriends had disappeared from her life after word got out about her and Will.

"We deserve at least this time together, don't we, Deb?"

"Yes."

But she didn't know if she could handle the part that came after. The pain of separating. She'd already done it once.

There'd always be an after—and it wouldn't bring them together. Not if they both went back to Buffalo.

"Amy's still on her study in Marseilles?" His voice asked about Amy, her roommate, but his eyes asked another question.

"Yes. Until Saturday."

It was Tuesday. They'd have four days to spend alone in her flat.

He stared at her, his face relaxed except for the sparkle in his eyes.

"Will—"

"You know how we'll end up, this week or next." He finished her thought. They had the whole semester ahead of them. In Paris...

"I just don't know if this is the best thing for us."

She damned the tears that threatened to spill, the quiver of her chin. It was as though they were fifteen and seventeen again and his mother had caught them kissing on the porch.

"We're not kids anymore. We're adults, Deb. Deb?"

His fingers touched her chin and forced her to look up. When she saw the same desire in his eyes that she felt every time they were together, her tears overflowed and dripped down her face, onto his hands.

"We'll never do anything you aren't comfortable with, Deb."

"That's not what I'm afraid of." She punched his arm. "And you know it."

Will's laugh chased away her fears. She didn't doubt the depth of her feelings for him, or his for her. It was the pain of letting go that they would both face, whether it was after this week or after a year in Paris.

They could never go back to Buffalo together.

CHAPTER NINE

Present Day
Buffalo, New York
Debra

WILL CHEWED his Thai spring roll, and his eyes met mine as I stared at him over my coconut-curry soup.

"What?" he asked. He tilted his head and set his fork down.

"Is something bothering you? You've been quiet since we left the house."

He swallowed.

"Nothing's bothering me. I'm just wondering how you're really doing with everything that's going on." He grabbed my left hand. "You're getting to the busiest part of your work, with the exhibit so close. Mama and Angie are giving you a lot to think about, and before we know it, Blair and Stella will be adding to our family, as well."

"I'm fine," I said. "Thrilled. Happy." I put down my spoon and covered our two hands with my right.

"Really?"

Will wasn't buying my cool composure. Neither was I, for that matter.

I let out a breath.

"Okay, I'm worried as hell. Angie's lucky to be living such a great life. I don't understand why she hasn't told her husband she's pregnant or why she didn't tell him she wants to stay here."

Will sighed. "Aw, honey, Angie's a big girl. We can't control the kids anymore."

"We never could, could we?"

"No, we couldn't, but something tells me you're just figuring that out now." His gaze said it all. "You *do* realize you've got to let this go and focus on your career?"

"I thought she'd listen to me—"

"I don't think this means she isn't listening, Deb. She's weighed the risks and doesn't want to tell Jesse she's pregnant while he's out in Iraq. I must admit I'd feel better if she told him, but still, it's none of our business."

"She's always been the most stubborn."

"Deb, you've got to stay out of this. It's Angie's life, Angie's baby. We're just the future grandparents."

Will's expression yielded that rare view into his emotions, a view I'd only seen a few times over our life together. It was a raw, tortured glimpse into his real self.

His most emotional self.

I remembered seeing this look when we were at Crystal Beach, right after his father died. I saw this same side of Will moments before he kissed me for the first time, when we were teenagers.

And again when the twins were born.

The most painful occasion for me to recall was

when he met Angie, when he learned he had a child—a daughter.

I still felt responsible for the hurt he'd suffered when he'd discovered he'd missed the birth of his own daughter. A hurt he recognized fully when the twins were born and he realized how much he'd missed.

So each time Will gave me this look, I knew it was an important moment. I was not always sure why, but I knew it was. It symbolized another milestone in our life together.

I wasn't ready for any more milestones. Not tonight.

"You're upset with me, aren't you?" I struggled to keep the agitation out of my voice.

"You have no idea." Will's annoyance with me was loud and clear.

"Why didn't you tell me?"

"It's not something I could articulate. Besides, it's not like I've never mentioned it. I have. You just happen to be listening this time."

"Listening to *what*, Will?"

"I've told you before. You're always apologizing for who you are."

"Who I am?"

"Who *we* are. Who we are together."

"Bull—"

He held up his hands, and not just to shove away his half-finished plate of lamb curry.

"No, it's not bull, Deb. You've spent our entire marriage making sure everyone else is happy, that everyone understands you don't hold their prejudice against them."

"That's not fair." Tears welled up. Why had Will picked a public place to stage such a personal discussion?

"You're right. It's *not* fair, Deb. It's not fair that you risked shortchanging our children, deny them the ability to deal with their heritage. Or that you've cheated yourself. You've cheated us."

"Us?"

His face had a drawn, resigned look.

"Yes. For once, Deb, it would be so nice to know you didn't give a damn about what that couple over there—" he motioned behind his shoulder "—thinks. Or these people." He pointed to the right of our table.

"I don't care what *anyone* else thinks! And in case you haven't noticed, our kids have turned out pretty darned well."

"No, on the surface you don't care. But deep down you've always felt we placed a burden on our kids. Did it ever occur to you that our family and what we've dealt with has made our kids better? Stronger?"

"Like my family did me?" The sarcastic tone of my voice destroyed any chance of resolving this peacefully at the restaurant table. Will knew it hurt me that I was essentially estranged from my mother.

I stood up and grabbed my purse.

I walked out into the parking lot of the restaurant and sucked in a deep breath. It was so cold it made me cough, which at least took my mind off the pain in my heart.

Will followed a few minutes later, after he'd paid the bill.

We got into his car without comment. Typical of Will and me—we threw our cards on the table, then let them lie there for a while.

It was like when I knitted up a sample swatch to see how a particular yarn looked with different stitches. I had to wait and work on another project for a bit before I knew if I wanted to move forward with a particular stitch and fiber combination.

Sometimes an old sweater that didn't fit anymore came back in style and I did the pattern again, in an updated yarn and often a larger size.

But our marriage wasn't a knitted garment. It was more like a wardrobe that spanned years, decades and, now, a generation.

We pulled into the garage. Will cut the engine and pressed the button on the automatic garage door opener. He turned to me.

"I'm not ready to continue this conversation, Deb. Can we just go in and get some rest?"

"Of course."

I stared at him, and he at me.

How are we still together?

The thought flitted across my mind as if it were a nursery rhyme instead of a potential grenade.

I'd loved Will forever and always would. But our compatibility wasn't perfect.

"Will—"

The light on the door opener clicked off. Since the garage was attached to the house and the one window faced the woods, we were plunged into darkness.

"Not now, Debra."

The dome light came on as Will opened his door and got out of the car. I had no choice but to follow.

"Easy for you to say," I muttered.

Will had never worried as I did. He felt the kids were so privileged financially and academically that any negative issues due to their obvious mixed-race background weren't significant.

"Hey, it's just as easy for me to *do*. But I know it's never been in your repertoire to let things fall as they may. Did it ever occur to you that the world goes on without Debra Bradley to keep it spinning?"

We entered the house, and Rose greeted us, tail wagging.

"I'll take her for a walk." Will collected Rose's leash.

Tears of frustration stung my eyelids.

"So we're back at it and you've been home, what, half a day?"

It angered me that he would come home and be so loving, only to turn on me later and try to get me to see things his way. When it came to the kids, we'd never seen eye-to-eye. Not a hundred percent, not even fifty.

I'd stayed home to raise them. So it made sense to me that I felt more protective of them on all counts.

"C'mon, Rosie." Will didn't reply, just clipped the leash on the dog's collar and went out through the front door.

I had a few minutes alone and was grateful for them. I needed to calm down. It didn't all have to be solved tonight.

By the time Will and Rose came back, I was sitting at the farmhouse table that stood between the kitchen and the family room.

"I made some chamomile." And I'd laced his with extra honey, the way he liked it. Maybe that would take the edge off.

"Thanks." He removed his coat and slipped out of his shoes.

"It's almost balmy out there. Rose splashed through the slush like she was at the beach."

I didn't comment. It was my turn to wait for him to settle in, to get a few sips of tea into his belly.

"I don't get it, Will. I'm not supposed to be emotionally invested in my own daughter's pregnancy? A daughter who hasn't even told her *husband* she's pregnant?"

Will set down his tea and looked at me. He was calmer than he'd been fifteen minutes earlier.

"Honey, you're beyond emotionally invested. You think everything that happens to any of our kids is because of you or me, something we did or didn't do."

"But I'm a parent, a mother."

"True, but this isn't about being a parent, Deb. It's about your need to feel in charge of everything. Hell, you wouldn't even think of marrying me until I all but begged you to. You thrive on control, imagined or not."

I blinked back tears. This was supposed to be a happy time for us. Angie had said it and she'd been right.

"It always goes back to that summer, those early years." My words came out in a strangled whisper.

"*Babe.* We've had a great ride together so far, and I'm looking forward to much more." Will reached under the table and squeezed my knee.

His eyes still twinkled, past the exhaustion and sorrow I saw in their depths.

"You asked, and I'm telling," he said. "Maybe I should've pushed you on this years ago, but I've always been so happy with you as my wife that I overlooked what I saw as your shame."

"Shame...of what?"

"The effect our blended genes would have on our kids. The fact that they're neither black nor white but both. The fact that it *may* have exposed them to prejudice or unfair treatment."

Pain seared through me.

"I love you, Will, and I love our children. I'm not ashamed of anything we've done together. God, everything I've done is for *all* of you."

"So do this one last thing for me and let it go, Deb. Let go of having to be the protector. Let go of having to be the one to fix everything. Because you can't, love. Sometimes what we think needs fixing isn't even broken."

I studied his blurred image through my wet eyes. Will's words hurt because they were true. I was reminded of a time when I'd had to confront Will about his relationship with his mother. That his concern for her was getting in the way of our love for each other.

"Is this how you felt when I told you that you had to stop trying to be everything for Vi?" It was hard to imagine that anything I'd ever said to Will had so deeply jarred him.

"Probably." Will didn't make any apologies for how he felt, or the words he'd spoken.

I knew my husband didn't talk about emotional issues unless pushed, or unless he thought it would help one or both of us.

"Why didn't you tell me you felt this way sooner?"

"I told you, honey, I've never been so unhappy that it mattered. But now our children are on their own. Isn't it time for you and me to be the couple we've always dreamed about?"

"We're not kids anymore, Will."

"No, but the kids we were wouldn't want us to waste this precious time together. Time we've waited a lifetime for."

I considered pointing out that we weren't alone, even now. His mother needed us, and she lived in the cottage behind our house.

But I kept my thoughts quiet. I didn't want Will to think for a moment that I had any issue with Vi's dependence on us. I treated her as I'd want my family to treat me in the same circumstance—with dignity and respect.

Still, I couldn't resist saying, "So much for a nice welcome-home celebration."

Will sighed. "Sometimes it's better just to get it out in the open, Deb. We're both good at shoving it down, ignoring what isn't pleasant or cozy. But we've had almost forty years together, more if you count when we met. I want the best years to be ahead of us, don't you?"

I stared at him.

"And your way of making the future 'the best years' *isn't* controlling? In your own way?"

I was unable to stop the flow of words.

"Deb, I'm not trying to change you, and I'm sorry you feel that I am. I love you. I'm happy, very happy. But I'm tired of the weight of this. I wish you could see what I see—you're beautiful and you have a wonderful

family who loves you. You don't need to take on everyone else's problems."

He put his hand on my arm. "It's weighing you
down, too, babe."

Will lifted his hand to pet Rose, whose muzzle rested
on his lap.

He raised his head and looked at me.

"I'm not even sure how I can help you do this, but
somehow you've got to learn to let go, Deb. We're too old
to be hanging on to anything other than our happiness."

February 1973
Paris, France

"I CAN'T FIND my key." Debra fumbled in her backpack,
her numb fingers not touching it.

"Here, let me." Will took the backpack from her and
reached in. His fingers had stayed warm during their
walk, since he wore the gloves she'd knitted him for
Valentine's Day.

"Here we go." She watched as he found her keychain
and inserted the key into the apartment door. Debra
liked that Will never said "I told you so." He'd suggested she put her own mittens on, but she'd preferred
to feel his hands through the merino wool of his gloves.

He held the door for her, waiting for her to pass. They
were both inside the small entryway, at the bottom of
the stairs that led up to her loft. Will shut the door, and
the silence descended upon them.

It was the first time they'd been alone in her apartment knowing they had hours, days, ahead of them.

"Hey." Will grasped her chin and raised her gaze to his. Her desire for him warmed her and excited her at the same time. But she had to laugh because Will—her charming, happy, studious Will—looked so serious.

"What's so funny?" His breath fanned the wisps of hair off her cheeks. She loved his smell.

"You seem so worried. It's not like you."

"Are you still okay with this?" Will stayed true to his nature and kept their focus on the situation at hand.

Deb swallowed, never losing eye contact with Will. She nodded. "More than ever."

Will studied her for a moment, then pushed himself away with what appeared to be great effort.

He looked upstairs.

"What's it take for a guy to get a cup of tea around here?"

She giggled. "C'mon."

They went upstairs.

"Do you have much studying this weekend?" he asked.

"No, just a paper that's due on Tuesday. But I've got it done."

She'd stayed up three nights this past week to finish the paper early. She was so excited at the prospect of spending the entire weekend alone with Will that she couldn't sleep much, anyhow.

"What about you?"

"I have an exam next Friday. That's it for now." The weekend stretched before them like a rainbow after a summer storm.

One huge glorious gift of time.

And solitude.

"I still can't believe we found each other again. In Paris."

"Me neither." She held her mug in both hands and stared at the fire they'd started. A great thing about old Parisian apartments was that they had fireplaces. Will had paid for the wood.

"Did you ever think of me?" Will's voice was tentative, almost vulnerable.

"After high school?" How much could she reveal to him? "Yes, I did. But I tried not to."

"Why?"

"Why? Because we couldn't do anything about it. We never stood a chance in Buffalo, not with both our families and all."

"And all" really meant his mother, but she didn't comment. He knew.

"I suppose so."

His mug clanked on the floor next to his feet as he set it down. Then he took her mug out of her hands and set it next to his. He traced his finger along her face. "I can't do this if I don't know you're in it all the way, sweetheart."

"Will, of course I am! But it's not just about us. It never has been."

"It is now, Deb. And it can be when we go back. We're adults, and we have our own life to live."

"You make it sound so simple."

"It *is* simple, when you get down to it."

"How—"

Her words were swallowed by Will's mouth as it covered hers. This kiss caught her a bit off guard. But it was as delicious as all the others had ever been. Even more so.

Everything in their past had been leading to this moment. She knew that now, as the intensity of their embrace deepened with each kiss, each caress. He pressed her back, until he was lying half across her on the sofa. Their kisses grew longer, and their breath quickened to match her crazy pulse.

Will lifted his head and looked into her eyes. She saw all the love and devotion he'd always had for her, and now could give to her with no restraint.

"I love you, Debra, and I'm going to prove it to you for the rest of our lives. If you let me."

"Oh, Will…"

CHAPTER TEN

Present Day
Buffalo, New York

Hɪ, Aɴɢᴇ,
As expected, I have little time to myself. Work is re-
warding and challenging. It was awkward when I left
since we both had a lot of pressure. Can we talk? I
can call when I get a lull in the O.R.
J.

Angie closed her laptop and stood up from her
kitchen table. All these weeks she'd checked her e-mail
every day, sometimes obsessively so. She'd longed for
a message, any kind of news from Jesse.

Her morning sickness was a normal part of pregnancy for sure, but her anxiety over his well-being
added to her stomach's bilious behavior.

The crabapple tree outside the kitchen window
waved its gnarled branches in the strong wind. It was
hard to imagine the pretty pink blossoms that would
cover it come spring.

Spring—she'd be in her second trimester by then.

Jesse deserved more from her. Maybe Mom was right; she should tell him sooner rather than later.

She looked at her watch. Her shift started in an hour.

As the new head meteorologist at the NOAA station, she alternated her day and night shifts so she'd get to know the entire staff and see how they worked. So far she was very impressed with how advanced their weather-predicting capabilities were.

Many television stations simply reported the weather as they received it from the nearest NOAA, with little or no interpretation by their own meteorologists. Due to the constant flux of Western New York's meteorological patterns, the station was heavily relied upon.

Her colleagues in San Francisco would be envious of her new position—and the challenges of lake-effect weather. They had to wait years between El Niño weather patterns.

She felt the relaxation in her facial muscles as her frown turned into a reluctant smile. She had her own El Niño, or La Niña, going on. Her e-mail alert chimed.

Hi, Ange,

I don't feel right about how we parted. I know we both said it was for the best, that we'd hit a wall. But I can't imagine life without you, Ange. And this isn't just because I'm over here, away from all the creature comforts of the U.S.A.

Can I call you?

I have to talk to you.

Ciao, Bella,

Jesse

So she was "Bella" again. He hadn't used that term of endearment the last time they spoke.

Jesse started calling her Bella after their trip to Tuscany last summer. They'd rented a villa for two weeks. It all blurred together in her mind—a collage of colorful meals, sunflower fields, medieval art and making love as the sun or moon rose.

It was a second honeymoon as far as Angie was concerned. That constant glow of contentment with each other, and the security that their love could last.

That it *would* last.

She sighed and went into the kitchen for some ginger tea. She and Jesse had gone through the holidays as always—visiting each other's families at Thanksgiving and Christmas and then spending New Year's Eve together in San Francisco.

They cherished what had become an annual tradition—curling up in front of their condo's fireplace with a spread of cheeses, sausages and a bottle of red wine. Most often it was wine they'd chosen on a day trip to Napa or Sonoma, but this year it had been a bottle they'd brought back from Italy. A wonderful Barolo they'd enjoyed in Piedmont.

She hadn't known she was pregnant at the time. But she'd only sipped at one glass, leaning against Jesse and forgetting for one night that the distance between them had been widening over the past few months.

She should've tried to talk to him then, before it was too late. To let him know how badly she wanted the position in Buffalo. And that she'd researched jobs for him, and—serendipitously—the top hospital in Western New York was looking for a chief of neurosurgery.

Jesse's dream job.

But she'd said nothing.

A week later it was too late. Jesse was on a plane to Iraq for an indeterminate length of time and she was left to make her own decision. Jesse knew she was coming to Buffalo but thought it was just to check out the job, assuming she probably wouldn't take it. Even though he insisted he was willing to accept a temporary position in neurosurgery in Buffalo after his return from Iraq, Angie knew he didn't expect her to make such a permanent change on her own. Pregnant or not.

With a feeling of recrimination she fought back her tears. These weren't hormonal tears. She should've told Jesse how she felt about the job on New Year's Eve.

But she'd just realized she'd missed her period by a week, something she'd never done. Motherhood was thrust upon her, and while she knew without a doubt that she'd have the baby and raise it alone if need be, she'd hoped and prayed that Jesse would change his mind about a family.

She never told him she was pregnant. Didn't want him to worry about her or carry any anger with him into such a hostile environment.

She was headed east on I-80 by the end of January. She lucked out with the weather and made it to Kansas ahead of a huge winter storm system. She'd had to wait it out in Kansas City for a few nights, but then continued to Buffalo without further delays.

So here she was. Back home, but it didn't feel like home. Not without Jesse.

She picked up the phone.

Of their own volition, it seemed, her fingers dialed her mom's number.

"Hello?"

Angie sighed with relief that Debra was home.

"Hey, Mom." Her voice broke on "Mom."

"What's wrong, sugar? Are your hormones driving you nuts?"

"Yeah, but it's more than that."

Debra was silent. Angie pictured her mother drawing invisible doodles on the table in front of her, as she did whenever her friends called with a problem.

Angie dove in. "Mom, I'm not whining. I'm an adult and I'm not the first woman in history to find herself pregnant at an unexpected time." She looked at her countertop, the hardwood floor. "I just thought that Jesse, well, that he'd, oh, crap. I thought I'd change him."

"You mean that he'd decide on his own that he wanted kids?"

Angie shoved down her twinge of guilt. "Something like that, yes."

"Angie, what has he said? That he absolutely *never* wants children?" Her mom's voice was gentle, not judging.

It was Angie's turn to be silent.

"Angie? Are you still there?"

"Yes, Mom. He still wasn't ready to discuss it before he left. That's why I didn't tell him."

Debra's intake of breath echoed through the receiver. "What were you thinking?" The old judgmental Mom was back.

"I didn't want him to feel trapped."

"You wanted him on your terms. Period."

"What's so wrong with that? That I want the father of my child to stay with me and be part of our family?"

"There's never been any question in my mind that Jesse loves you and wants to be with you, Angie. He had such a rough time as a kid, from what you've told me, that it's no wonder he wasn't prepared to commit to children. Not right away."

Angie didn't say anything.

She heard rhythmic clicking over the phone. Mom must have resumed her knitting. "You didn't have any problem with this before."

"Yeah, well, I wasn't knocked up before." Angie knew Debra hated harsh talk.

"Excuse me, but you're carrying my grandchild. Don't refer to yourself as 'knocked up.'"

"Sorry I bothered you, Mom. I just needed to vent, I suppose."

"You're not bothering me." The clicking ceased. "I'm here for you, Angie. But I also respect that this is your life."

Angie couldn't find words to respond. Her mother had never said anything remotely akin to suggesting any of the kids were capable of leading their own lives. Since when had Debra Bradley learned about emotional boundaries?

"Uh, thanks, Mom."

"Anytime, sugar. Just try to stay off the pity pot, okay?"

"Yeah."

"When do you go back to work?"

"Later this evening."

"You're not used to having extra time on your hands. You haven't had a chance to make friends yet, and what have you done besides work?"

"Not much." She enjoyed her own knitting and crocheting, but hadn't found much incentive to pick it up again.

"Do something nice for yourself. Tell you what, why don't I book us in at La Spa and we'll spend an afternoon together?"

"I don't know how much of it I could enjoy right now, Mom."

"I get it. We don't want you to throw up during a massage." Debra's husky laugh made Angie smile. "Okay, honey. Just get out of that apartment and do *something*."

"All right. Thanks, Mom. Bye."

"Bye."

Angie set the portable phone down and sipped her tea. It was lukewarm now but still soothed her gag-prone throat. She ran her finger around the rim of the hand-thrown mug.

It wasn't fair to drag Mom into all her life's snarls. She'd tied her own knots; she'd untie them, too.

Present Day
Buffalo, New York
Debra

THE OLD BROWN SWEATER felt rough against my fingers. I'd made two of them for the boys when they were six and playing soccer.

I'd only managed to save this one. I didn't know where the other one went.

The acrylic-wool blend wasn't anything I'd use today, but it served its purpose for two boys in the Buffalo winter. The soccer ball motif on the front had been difficult but "anything for the kids" had been my motto.

Will wasn't wrong about that.

I brought the sweater to my face and breathed in its scent. Past the lavender oil I used to protect the sweaters from moths, I caught a whiff of Blair and Brian when I was the only woman in their lives, other than their grandmas. I remembered slush dragged into the house on rubber boots, cold skin after soccer practice in the rain.

The constant observation of the other kids' parents, especially the mothers.

At times I missed having young boys in the house but I didn't miss the intrusion of other people's opinions....

CHAPTER ELEVEN

Present Day
Buffalo, New York
Debra

I PUT THE BROWN sweater to the side, into the pile of items I might use in my exhibit. I certainly had enough to fill an entire showroom. But I wanted this to be more than another open-portfolio type of show. I wanted to tie my work and art in with history.

I recalled Shirley's words. "You of all people have something to scrapbook about."

The thought of displaying personal things I'd made, not just the public weavings and tapestries, in the art exhibit, made me feel vulnerable to the criticism of others. What if the reviewers and the public didn't understand my motives? I wanted to show how real life, ordinary life, continues even when national and international situations are globe-altering.

The baby and toddler clothes I knitted for Angie during the Watergate hearings.

The things I knitted for Will when we were in high school and college, when the civil rights movement brought racial violence I'd never known about. When I understood that civil rights wasn't just about some black people on television. It was about Will and me and all of us.

I'd loved Will since I first saw him on the bus. Since he took me under his arm and watched out for me, all through elementary and middle school. Even after we stopped seeing each other in high school I still loved him.

The pain of losing my best friend, Will, was almost worse than thinking I'd lost his love completely.

It was not that I'd always been colorblind, either. Sure, as kids, I knew we had different skin. As we grew up and closer together, Will's blackness was attractive to me because it was part of who he was.

It was part of us.

I sat in my studio at the desk where I'd laid out all the photographs I'd been gathering for the past few months. Starting with the late 1950s until the present day, I'd collected world, national and local news headlines.

My original plan had been to display the news items on boards behind each piece of artwork I'd done at that particular time.

The museum wanted a retrospective of my art, how I'd gotten where I was today. So although I thought it a bit frivolous, I was going to include some small weavings I'd done as a child in elementary art class. Before I ever knew fiber arts could yield a career for me.

An entire vocation, for that matter.

I sighed and sipped my tea. My chipped mug was the

only warm thing in my studio. The news images stared blankly at me. Even my knitting didn't seem as inviting as I'd hoped it would be.

"Nonsense." I spoke to myself and Rose, who merely thumped her tail as she lay curled up in her bed. I was letting all that talk about journaling and scrapbooking get to me.

Not every life could be captured on a heartwarming scrapbook page.

Especially mine.

April 1985
Buffalo, New York

"BRIAN, PUT YOUR SHIRT ON. Blair, are your shin guards in place?"

Debra twisted around in the station wagon and surveyed the backseat. Both boys were in a state of undress as they rushed to get ready for the soccer game.

Angie was at ballet—Debra had to pick her up in thirty minutes—and her main focus was getting the boys to their field. She'd get Angie and be back before the game ended.

"Mom!"

They protested in unison. She knew she could be repetitive, but they needed the prodding. It'd been all she could do to get them into the car after school.

They'd chased each other around the parking lot, oblivious to Debra's words of caution.

One old wives' tale about twins that Debra had found to be true for Blair and Brian was that they lived in their own world. Not only did they have their own language, she swore they communicated telepathically with each other at times.

"Take your water bottles."

A tap on the window startled Debra. She rolled it down and Doug Bartholomew's handsome face obstructed her view of the pitch.

"Need a hand?"

His wide smile crinkled the tanned skin around his eyes just a little too perfectly. People in Buffalo didn't have tans like that unless they wintered in the tropics or went to a tanning salon. She was pretty sure Doug fell into the latter category.

"Nope, we're ready, boys, aren't we?" She looked back into the car, avoiding the forced intimacy the rain and his presence created.

"See ya, Mom." Brian opened his door and slipped out. Blair slid across the car seat and let himself out the same door.

"They sure do everything together, don't they?"

Debra turned to face Doug.

His blue eyes revealed the loneliness that lurked behind the bravado.

"Yes, they do. I'm getting out, too."

She pulled on her door handle and Doug stepped back. She decided to leave the umbrella in the car and zipped up her parka, pulling the hood over her head, although it was impossible to keep all the red curls inside it.

She fell into step beside Doug, who showed up at all the soccer games. His wife, Mina, was a real estate agent, one of the most successful in Western New York.

Doug was an optometrist, so he arranged his patients around his son's after-school schedule. It was easier for him than for Mina, he always said.

Debra often thought that maybe Doug and Mina didn't really like each other and welcomed the break. One of those in-name-only marriages.

"How's your project coming along?" He never forgot to ask about her fiber arts.

"Great, thanks. I wish I had more time with it, or at least bigger chunks of solid time, but, well, you know how it is with the kids."

"I've told you, Debra, whenever you want me to take the twins for an afternoon, just give me a call. Sam loves them and they get along well."

"Thanks, but they're not the problem. It's my time-management skills, which leave a bit to be desired."

Doug was correct; the boys all got along wonderfully. But she didn't want a man other than Will spending that much time with them. Due to Will's long hours, if she took Doug up on his offer, he'd see more of the twins than their own father did.

It didn't sit right with her.

"How's *your* work going?" She wanted to get him talking about himself. Maybe he'd lay off the personal questions.

"Not bad. I could use a few more clients but they'll come."

"How about Mina?"

"She's always doing great. You know her, never a slow day."

Actually, Debra didn't know Mina very well. They'd

only met a handful of times. Doug often had a gaggle of other soccer moms around him, laughing and flirting.

Mina didn't seem to mind that Doug received so much attention from other women. She'd once commented that she was relieved Doug had other women to "joke" with. Debra heard the undertone of hard knowing in Mina's voice. She knew her husband played around.

Debra figured Mina had confided in her because in Mina's eyes she was "different" from the other moms. She wasn't a threat because no white man would be interested in a white woman who'd married a black man.

Even though none of these thoughts were spoken aloud, Debra knew they existed. It was in the stares of the other moms as they noted the twins, often the only dark-skinned boys on the suburban teams. Then they'd search for the parents, and someone would have to point Debra out.

She wondered if they knew how stupid they looked with their open mouths when they saw her fair skin and red hair.

Doug had always been nice to her, but she didn't trust him, either. Debra knew she'd never approve of Will having a close friendship with another woman unless she was a friend of hers, too. Even then it was a questionable proposition.

They reached the field and the game started. Debra enjoyed laughing in the cold wet mess of a Buffalo autumn as she watched Blair and Brian chase the ball across the field.

It was similar to the joy she felt when she watched Angie at ballet. But with the boys it always seemed to involve some type of infectious fun. Even the other parents laughed at the boys' knack for getting each other out of tough spots.

"It's good to see you laugh." Doug stood a little too close for Debra's comfort.

"It feels good to laugh." She took a step to the side, and cupped her hands around her mouth. "Go, Brian! Go, Blair!"

Doug shook his head. "I hope your husband appreciates everything you do."

Debra heard the insinuation in his tone.

"Oh, he does, believe me." She set a stern boundary with her words, and this time Doug seemed to have heard her. He focused on the game again and refrained from any more personal comments or questions.

Deb sighed. She occasionally resented Will's long hours, and the fact that he missed so much of this time with the boys. But mostly she felt sad for him. He didn't have a choice at this point in their lives.

Besides, they needed her to stay home and be available for the children. And her fiber arts work was more flexible, although it often meant she was up past midnight or awake before the birds. But at least she had the option of working her own hours.

Will was following the classic claw-your-way-to-the-top career path. It took more than talent to be a successful architect. He had to be there, attend meetings, socialize with clients.

Big dreams were part of Will's being. He wanted his

firm to be the number-one firm for their specialty in the country.

Debra smiled to herself as she watched the twins compete, with their unique fierceness, on the field. She knew where *that* trait had come from.

CHAPTER TWELVE

Present Day
Buffalo, New York
Debra

I CHECKED ON THE EGGS I was poaching for Violet and pulled out the coffee to make a pot. Will was still in the shower. He'd decided to work out before he left for the office, in the little gym he'd made for us two years ago.

I preferred the elliptical trainer and stationary bike, while Will usually put time in on the treadmill. Will was happiest running outside, but the weather was hopeless this morning. The three inches of snow that fell two days ago had turned into slush due to a warm front. The temperature was going to drop to below zero after night-fall, guaranteeing an icy mess.

The phone rang and I picked it up while I took the eggs off the stovetop.

Caller ID said it was Angie.

"Good morning, sweetheart."

"Mom, have you seen the news?"

"No, I'm making breakfast for your father and grandmother. Do you mean the weather report? I saw that it predicts lower temperatures later. What's the problem?"

"I'm at work already. There's a storm front coming in from the plains, and an arctic current dipping south from Canada. The last time those conditions converged we had four feet of snow in twelve hours."

I heard the stress in Angie's voice as I looked through the kitchen window to the pale sunrise over the backyard. Dim shafts of light were just starting to appear in the woods.

"It's not snowing yet."

"No, but it will be by this afternoon. Make sure you and Daddy are stocked up on everything and tell him to work at home today."

"Too late. He's getting ready for a big conference call with Seattle and Toronto."

"He needs to get home right after lunch, then. City hall's going to shut down offices at noon."

"You know your dad, honey. He's got his four-wheel drive, and he does what he pleases."

"Mom." She was thirty-five but in some ways still the high-strung adolescent.

"Okay, okay." I shifted the phone to my other shoulder as I grabbed the salt and pepper shakers. "What about you? Are you going home early?"

"I'm hoping to stay over. This is a huge news event and the local stations are relying on us for the latest. I'm running home right now to get a few things. I was in such a hurry to leave this morning I forgot to pack an overnight bag."

I heard the excitement, but also fatigue, in her voice.

"How are you feeling today, Angie?"

"Better. Kind of. It's almost fourteen weeks, so I feel more like my old self."

"Call me when you get home, or at least check in so I know you're safe."

"Okay, bye, Mom."

"Bye."

I was proud of myself. I didn't remind Angie that she'd never be back to her "old self," not really. Angie would figure it out soon enough. Motherhood was forever.

The back door slid open and Violet walked in. Despite her eighty-five years and her cane, she still walked with the certainty of a confident woman.

"Good morning, Violet." I let the practiced chipper greeting flow off my tongue.

"Not going to be good for long if my arthritis is anything to judge by."

"I'm sorry you're hurting, Vi."

"Yes, yes." She waved her hands as if fending me off. "Before you ask, I started a double dose last night when the bones woke me up."

Besides heart disease, Violet had arthritis. Most days she did fine with her maintenance medication plan, but every now and then she needed more to ease the aches. A major weather front was enough to trigger a painful few days.

Her congestive heart failure had been managed so far with a pacemaker, defibrillator and regular medical attention. But it was always in the back of my mind that one day we wouldn't be able to stop its progression.

I poured Violet her special blend of coffee—half caffeinated, half decaf.

"Thanks." Her crooked fingers wrapped around the steaming mug.

"You're welcome."

I took a private moment to appreciate the small exchange of pleasantries. It wasn't always this comfortable between us.

As I slid out a kitchen chair for her, I noticed that her face looked a little more drawn than usual. Rather than ask about it, I made a mental note to keep an even closer eye on her.

"According to Angie there's a big weather system headed over the lake today. Your bones are right."

"She went through how many years of college to figure out what I already know?" Violet laughed and patted the table.

Violet's white hair, what was left of it, wisped around her fine-boned face. Her skin, once almost as mocha as Will's, had faded to a pale tan. But her eyes remained bright, alert and didn't miss a trick. Not for the first time I hoped Will had inherited his mother's genes instead of his father's. I wanted him around for many years to come.

I laughed and served Violet's and Will's breakfast.

"You have a point there, Vi."

A whiff of fine cologne caught my attention a split second before Will entered the kitchen.

"Mmm, that smells great, honey." He gave me a peck on the cheek. Even after all these years he was still careful not to be too demonstrative around his mother.

"Morning, Mama." Will bent to kiss his mother's

cheek. I saw how her face lit up whenever he showed her affection.

I understood the bond. I had it with the twins.

But in a more easygoing manner, I liked to think. Never as controlling as Vi had been—and still tried to be.

"Angie called."

"I'll bet she did." Will poured himself some orange juice. "I saw the news upstairs when I was getting dressed. It's going to be a doozy of a storm."

"Can't you cancel your meeting?"

His answer was reflected in his face before he spoke.

"Are you kidding? These are the key players in the Niagara deal. After today we'll be able to sign all the papers and break ground as soon as it thaws."

Will was referring to his current project. The new Grand Niagara Center was going to be located on both the U.S. and Canadian sides of the border, with only the falls separating the buildings. They'd attract a legion of high-end stores and successful businesses and bring in substantial income for both cities. Will had even been featured in *Forbes* magazine for this particular project.

"What's the earliest you'll be done?" I worried about him on the roads but didn't want to say so, not after last night's conversation. Will thought I was too protective as it was.

"Don't worry, it'll be early enough. This storm isn't supposed to get going until closer to midnight, and I'll be home long before then. Don't forget, the weather guessers aren't always right."

"Hey, your daughter's a 'weather guesser.' Don't let

her hear you say that!" I smiled at him. "Just make sure you're home before it gets too bad, Will. Violet, once the winds pick up—"

"I know, I'll bed down over here. But honestly, my cottage is fine. I'm warm there and it's never lost power yet."

"There's always a first time, Vi."

"Deb's right, Mama. You come over here when the snow starts. Better yet, why don't you stay at the house today?"

Will looked at his mother, to make sure he had her attention. "No long walks, Mama. Use the treadmill."

"It's too messy out there to walk anyhow." Vi clasped her coffee mug, and I saw the emotions flow across her face. She'd become easier to read as she aged, as though the layers were disappearing one by one.

She wasn't happy about having to stay at the house through the storm, but I knew she'd do it.

Vi hated to impose, but at this point she wasn't an imposition at all. She enjoyed her television programs and had a love of reading that kept her occupied. She also loved to cook, and if it was up to Vi, both Will and I would weigh a third more than we already did.

Will finished his breakfast and stood, stretching his arms overhead.

"That was great, honey."

"I could've made you canned stew and you'd love it. You'll eat anything after a workout."

"As long as you or Mama cooked it."

I walked Will to the front door. He leaned in close and whispered to me.

"You'll be okay with Mama here all day? Any chance you'll need to go out for groceries?"

"We have plenty. You know she doesn't bother me in the least." Will and I had kept an emotional distance since last night, but we'd been together too long to allow anything to get in the way of being affectionate.

Disagreements would work themselves out. Why miss any loving in the meantime?

I wound my arms around his neck.

"I'd love it if we have to snuggle up tonight to keep warm," I whispered.

Will lowered his mouth to mine and kissed me until I couldn't help leaning into him.

"Count on it, Deb."

I pressed my forehead to his chin. "Will, I'm sorry about everything."

"I didn't tell you so you could be sorry, Deb. I just want you to start enjoying *your* life. *Our* life."

I hugged him tight. "I'll miss you today."

"I'll miss you, too."

He let me go and opened the door. He buttoned up his coat, then put on his gloves.

"See you later."

I smiled as I put his hat on his head and gave him one last peck on the cheek.

"Bye."

Will strode under the portico and into the garage. He hadn't wanted the garage to open into the house. It was just one of many details he'd seen to when he'd drawn up the plans. We both liked the house being its own separate building.

Once Will left for work, my next task was to get Violet busy with something so I could work on my textile exhibit. And to try to keep my mind off Will's accusations last night.

CHAPTER THIRTEEN

July 1973
Buffalo, New York

DEBRA SLAPPED at a mosquito on her forearm. The mugginess of the summer night pressed against her.

"You're not eating your burger." Will usually devoured two of the sirloin burgers at their favorite local hangout. One of the few places they could go without being given second glances. It was a quaint mom-and-pop place in the heart of downtown Buffalo.

It had been a long, hot day as she worked in the tiny restaurant kitchen at Buddy's grill. Her thoughts of Will and her anticipation of seeing him after her shift were all that had kept her going.

Will wouldn't meet her eyes and his shoulders were hunched. Not typical for him.

"I have to tell you something."

Debra stopped sipping her vanilla-orange milkshake and sat up straighter. Normally she was the one who needed loosening up. She tended to take their relationship, and the fact that they were from such different backgrounds, far too seriously for Will. Even if they'd been of the same race, the disparity in their economic status was more than enough to make a long-term relationship impossible. At least in the eyes of their parents.

"What is it?" Shivers went down her spine and they weren't from the ice cream.

"My parents aren't going to take it well, Debra. The wedding."

"Will, we haven't even picked a date yet. They'll get used—"

"No, no, they won't."

"You mean your mother won't."

Will sighed and played absently with a French fry.

"She needs time." His voice was gravelly and low, deeper than its ordinary baritone.

Debra stared at Will's face, his handsome features drawn into a big frown.

"This isn't fair to you, Will," she began. "Have you ever thought about that? This is your time to spread your wings and see where your talent and education will take you. Instead you're being forced to fight your parents over who you're going to marry."

"You're right, but they've given me everything I have. I owe them."

For once she was grateful she'd gotten through college on scholarships and hard work alone. She didn't feel she owed anyone—other than herself. She'd do her best, but it would be on her own terms.

"You don't owe them your happiness, Will."

Will didn't say anything.

Realization hit Debra as painfully as if he'd punched her in the gut.

"You're having second thoughts." Her words came out in a whisper.

Will's mouth tightened into a firm line. He expelled a long breath, then took Debra's hands in his.

His eyes shone with the love she knew he felt for her, but also with regret. Sorrow.

"I've never second-guessed us, our love, my love for you. But our timing isn't good, Debra. You still have to finish a year of school, and my dad's business hasn't been doing so well. He's more tired these days, and he needs me to help him."

Will stroked her cheek.

"I'm not saying we can't get married. I do think we should slow it down, worry about a wedding later on."

"We weren't talking any earlier than next summer, Will, after I graduate."

Almost a year away.

It felt eons away, and now Will wanted to add more time?

"Let's just focus on now and getting you graduated next year."

Debra's tears plopped onto Will's hands and the table between them.

She pulled back but Will wouldn't allow her to let go of his hands.

"Deb, I love you. That hasn't changed."

"Clean it up, people." A ruddy-faced diner a few tables over didn't look at them but the comment couldn't have come from anywhere else. There were only the three of them in this corner of the outdoor eating area. Will and Debra hadn't done anything untoward or even slightly offensive. If they'd been a white couple the man wouldn't have made his comment. This type of subtle racism was the hardest for both of them, but especially Will.

Will scowled, and Debra moved her hands down to his forearms.

"Forget it, Will."

"I'm tired of forgetting things." She saw the anger in his eyes, and it wasn't solely at the ignorant man and his bigotry.

Will might be tired of forgetting things but he seemed willing to forget their chance at happiness.

Fatigue overwhelmed her. She'd had a long day at the restaurant and a wedding to cater tomorrow. She looked at Will. His expression had grown stony.

"Can we go?" she asked.

"Sure."

Will drove her home in silence. Debra kissed him chastely on the cheek and slid out of the front seat of his Thunderbird, a gift from his parents.

"I love you, Will."

She didn't wait for his reply. She had to get out of the car, through the kitchen, past her mother and to the privacy of her own room.

But her mother, Linda, proved to be a nonissue, as she wasn't home from Wednesday-night bingo yet.

Debra got herself a tall glass of water and took it up to her room. Once she lay flat on her bed, a numbing exhaustion overcame her. The ache in her chest welled up and she let the sobs come out.

If she and Will couldn't get past basic problems like

their parents' disapproval, how were they going to get through life together? How would they make it over the long haul? Debra hoped and believed that each year would open up more minds, and interracial relationships would become more accepted. But it wasn't going to be easy. They still had to get through today.

And today they wanted to settle in Buffalo, near both of their families. She didn't think it could ever happen. Not now.

Buffalo wasn't Paris.

WILL POUNDED on the steering wheel. He loved this car but hated what it stood for. Another bribe, another insidious tie to his parents' power and control.

He drove slowly and carefully through Debra's neighborhood and over to his own. He kept going past his parents' home. He couldn't go in yet. He still had to think.

He hadn't told Debra the half of it. His mother's hysterics, his father's glowering. He suspected his father had less of a problem with him loving a white woman than upsetting his mother.

Oh, his mother.

Violet had been raised by a strict woman who'd preached the gospel of elitism to her from childhood. Her social and financial status was irrefutable and she'd never be happy with any of her children marrying "below" it.

Violet had never liked Debra, ever since they were kids. She didn't like Debra's upbringing. Even with the promise of an Ivy League degree, Debra simply wasn't good enough for her Will.

Violet had never given up on Will marrying Sarah.

It hadn't helped that Sarah kept herself in the picture, acting as though Will was just going through a phase he'd get over at any moment. That he'd come to his senses, marry her, and all would be well.

He needed to talk to his parents again, more sternly this time. But first he had to talk to Sarah and make it perfectly clear that they had no future together. Period.

"WILL?" SARAH'S FATHER stood in the doorway. Will peered around his stout frame and into the parlor. Sarah sat on the couch with her mother, watching TV.

"Will!" Sarah had heard her father's voice and jumped up behind him. "Daddy, let him in."

"Actually, I just need to talk to you for a minute, Sarah. Can you come out here?"

If Sarah's dad could have leveled Will with his stare he would have.

"I'll be in here, Sarah." He gave Will another withering look before he allowed Sarah past him onto the porch.

Once Will had Sarah in front of him, he got right to the point. He had no doubt Sarah's entire family was listening through the screen windows, but he didn't care. The heat and his frustration made privacy less important than setting the record straight.

"Sarah."

"Will, this is a surprise." She smiled at him, pouting just a little. He might have surprised her, but Sarah was never without an attempt to hook him.

"Look, Sarah, it's clear to me that my mother's been

leading you on about my feelings toward you. I have to let you know that while I enjoyed our few dates several years ago, I have no intention of pursuing this. You deserve the truth. You should start looking for someone else."

Sarah's eyes narrowed. "That white girl's got you by the nose, doesn't she, Will?" Her pretty face was twisted with ugly bigotry.

"Debra is my future wife. And I'm in love with her. Of my own free will."

He kept his gaze steady. Sarah had to understand that his mother was out of line. But he wasn't going to be disrespectful to Violet if he didn't have to. Sarah was an adult; she knew the deal.

"What happens when it doesn't work out, Will? When the taboo of loving someone you shouldn't wears off and she leaves you? And how fair are you being to your future children, Will? Have you really thought about this? Do you want some spotted—"

"That's enough, Sarah. I didn't come here to ask your opinion or your permission. I'm just telling you to back off. There's not going to be a 'you and me.' Ever."

"Will, I'm sorry. I got carried away. You know it's only because I care."

"If you care, Sarah, you'll stop talking to my mother and leave me be."

"Fine."

"Thanks again for your time."

"Goodbye, Will." Sarah sniffed, but Will didn't stay around to see her go back into the house. He had one more confrontation tonight.

CHAPTER FOURTEEN

Present Day
Buffalo, New York

WILL'S DRIVE TO THE OFFICE was uneventful, despite the slushy mess on the streets. The skies were growing darker, he noted, and the air was already getting chillier. That storm was definitely on its way.

He turned into his spot in the parking garage and killed the engine. He sat for a moment, gathering his thoughts. His love for Debra and the kids was unquestionable, and he knew Debra understood that. Yet there were times in a marriage when one of them had to speak up, to keep the other on track.

Deb had kept him on track through so much. She'd even bridged the chasm his father's death had created between him and his mother.

But now it was his turn to keep her on track. Some time ago Deb had decided she knew best for everyone in the family. He hadn't paid much attention. He'd been too busy with his career.

Now Debra had a chance to really shine with her own career accomplishments, but she still distracted herself from her work with the kids' problems and concerns.

She'd seemed crushed last night when he'd told her how he felt—that she'd been ashamed after all these years of their mixed marriage.

He shook his head. *Ashamed* wasn't the right word. Apologetic, maybe?

His watch beeped as it did on the hour, every hour. The teleconference was in thirty minutes.

He'd reopen the discussion with Debra when he got home.

July 1973
Buffalo, New York

WILL DROVE UP his parents' driveway, knowing this could be the last time he'd come to their house. After he told his parents his intentions, he knew his father would kick him out for upsetting his mother, and his mother would disown him.

So be it.

He parked in front of the house he'd been raised in. It was a good house. It had been fun when he was younger, with him and his little sister and brother running through the halls, playing hide-and-seek in all the closets and even on the dumbwaiter.

The house was almost two hundred years old. His dad had kept up with renovations and repairs over the years, but in the past while, there'd been more of a strain on the family budget, with his younger siblings in college and now Doreen getting married.

She was getting married at age twenty-one, three days after her graduation from Hampton University. His parents should be more concerned about Doreen marrying that sly dog Thomas than his marriage to Debra. He and Debra were well-suited, emotionally and intellectually. Doreen and Thomas, however, were two spoiled, immature kids who still expected everything to be handed to them. They even expected their parents to help with their first home and, sure enough, Mom and Dad had donated to the cause.

Will growled to himself. He wasn't asking his parents for a dime. He just wanted their love and understanding.

He'd always been the dutiful oldest son, taking care of the younger kids and still getting the best grades, achieving whatever challenge was presented to him.

Yet now it seemed none of that mattered. He should've screwed off and had more fun if it was all going to come to this anyhow. It would've been a lot more entertaining to be the prodigal son.

He found Mom in his parents' room. It was really his mother's room; his dad merely slept there. Purple flowers, Violet's namesake, dotted the wallpaper. His mother sat in her lavender easy chair, reading one of her beloved mystery novels.

"Will! I didn't expect you back so soon." Was that a spark of hope in her eyes that he'd broken off his date with Debra?

"Where's Dad?"

"In the bathroom. His stomach's acting up again." Will's gaze took in the closed bathroom door.

"Dad!"

"In a minute!" The muted response was clear even through the thick oak.

"What's got you all riled up?" Violet Bradley thought she could solve the world's problems, including Will's, with a motherly chat.

"It's time we settled something, Mama. I was at Sarah's tonight—"

"You were?" Anticipation flared in Violet's eyes.

"Yes, but it's not for the reason you want, Mom. I don't love Sarah. I don't even *like* her all that much. We have nothing in common. It's wrong of you to lead her on and encourage her infatuation. She doesn't even know the real me."

"But she could learn to." Violet's equanimity stirred his anger to the breaking point.

"No, Mother. No!" He clenched his fists. "You've done nothing but try to control my life, especially my love life, since I was in high school." He took a step toward her. "Well, it's done, Mother. I'm in love with Debra and I'm going to marry her."

As the words came out of his mouth and hung in the air, he watched his mother gasp, pale, then flush with fury. Her gaze drilled daggers into his heart, but Will was prepared. His lifetime happiness depended on it.

"Listen here, son. If it wasn't for your father and me you wouldn't have met this girl you think you're in love with. I should've cut her out of the picture long ago. I never should've let you play together." Violet crossed her arms.

"How, Mom? By locking me in my room every day after school? By not allowing Daddy to hire Deb's mother?"

The bathroom door opened and Will's dad strode out. "What's going on?"

"Will's crazy, William. He says he's marrying that, that who—"

"Mother! You don't have to like it but I will not have you talking about my future wife like this."

"Hold on a minute." William looked from Will to Violet and his gaze stayed on Violet.

"Since when did your relationship get to such a serious point?"

"It's always been serious, Dad. You two just didn't want to admit it." Will stood in front of both his parents, his hands reaching out to them.

"Ever since Mom scared the hell out of Debra when we were together on the front porch, we've all denied the truth—the truth that this is the woman I'm meant to be with, to marry. To have children with."

When Will uttered the word *children* Violet cried out and clutched her chest.

"Oh, my-God-sweet-Lord-in-heaven, you don't know what you're doing, Will! You're too young to know the consequences of your actions."

"I'm not a kid anymore. You have to accept that."

"Don't tell your mother what she has to accept or not, Will. I, uh—" William gasped for air and grabbed at his chest. But it wasn't for dramatic effect.

"Dad? Dad!"

"William!"

Will ran the few steps to his father and eased him to the ground.

"I can't, I can't—" William Bradley kept gasping for

breath and trying to talk, but wasn't managing to do either.

"It's okay, Dad, we're here." Will undid his dad's pajama top as he spoke.

"Mom, call the operator! Get an ambulance!"

Violet, shocked into a frozen stare, snapped out of it and picked up the white bedroom phone.

"Dad, can you hear me?"

His father looked up at Will.

"…love you…take care of your mother, son." William's face stilled, his expression half pained, half surprised. When his father exhaled a final time, and the foam seeped from his mouth, Will knew his mother's strident call for an ambulance didn't matter anymore.

CHAPTER FIFTEEN

July 1973
Buffalo, New York

DEBRA HAD DOZED OFF by the time her mother got back from bingo, but Linda woke her up. Debra opened her eyes to the sight of her mother leaning against the doorjamb.

"Will's mother called."

"Here?" Deb rubbed her eyelids and forced herself to sit up.

Violet Bradley had never made any attempt to contact Debra or her mother. She'd never even spoken to Debra's mother except in passing at the doctor's office, years ago. Linda had worked as a receptionist at a law firm for the past ten years.

Linda eyed her through the haze of her cigarette smoke. Earlier Debra couldn't wait to get out of the restaurant kitchen and the smell of burning oil and garlic. Now she longed for it.

"Will's father died. Heart attack."

"No." The word came out on the exhalation of her breath. Quick, shocked.

Debra got out of bed and followed her mother into the kitchen. She sank into the worn vinyl-covered chair across the table from where her mother sat.

For once, the Formica table was comforting in its familiarity. Her elbows stuck to the plastic surface and Debra wondered why she was focusing on physical details when Will's father was dead.

Dr. Bradley *gone?*

He was larger than life, the rock of Will's family. He'd given Debra's mother a lifesaving job. He'd been Debra's hope for change in all matters involving Violet.

And he was dead.

"She doesn't like you, Debbie. Her husband just died, but all she did was spit venom about you. What on earth did you do to her?"

"What did I do to her? Mother, she's hated me since the day I met Will."

Linda took a long drag on her cigarette and blew it out her nose.

"You're young. You'll have good sex with other men. Will isn't the right choice for you. Why don't you just accept it?"

Debra said nothing. Leave it to her mother to reduce everything to sex or money. The lowest common denominators.

She had two weeks left in this house before she'd be gone forever. Back to college for the year, then beginning a career next summer. She'd hoped it was going to be with Will.

It sure as hell wasn't going to be in Buffalo.

"What else did she say, Mother?"

"She told me to keep my daughter away from her precious son." Linda stubbed out her cigarette and lit up another. Her mother put chain-smoking on turbo speed.

"Trust me, Debbie, you don't want to go into a marriage with a mother-in-law like that. She'll ruin anything you have between the two of you."

"I can't deal with this right now."

Debra grabbed her purse from where she'd dropped it on the floor.

"Don't wait up, Mom."

The last was a purposeful jibe as Linda never waited up for Debra. Her beauty sleep was too important.

THE LIGHTS IN THE Baptist church reflected off the cream walls like tiny halos. Chandeliers hung over the main aisle, which was carpeted in red. At the end of the carpet, in front of the altar, was a smooth, ebony casket with gold handles and trim.

No one noticed Debra when she slipped in, as the service had started. She arrived late to avoid any unnecessary attention drawn to her or, more importantly, Will.

She could make out his form as he sat next to his mother with his siblings flanking either side of them. She had to come just so Will would know she was here. And that she loved him through thick and thin.

The pastor gave a beautiful eulogy. He'd obviously known Will's family for a long time. Debra wasn't used to a church service other than the Mass she attended weekly, but she enjoyed the warmth and obvious faith that united this community.

So moved was she that she didn't think twice about going up to the casket to say goodbye to Will's father, and to offer him a private thank-you for being such a great dad to Will.

She approached the casket as part of the slow line that reached to the back of the church, allowing the other mourners to take time with their final farewells.

When she arrived at the casket she looked down at the face that was so similar to Will's. The handsome profile, the full head of hair. She closed her eyes and held her hand to his hands. They were cold, of course, but it gave Debra a sense of strength and peace she hadn't had this entire summer.

The shriek that erupted behind her made her eyes fly open and she instinctively flinched. Hard blows rained down on her back and she turned to find Will, his brother and his sister pulling Violet away from her. Violet's eyes blazed with rage.

"Leave my family alone and go back to your white-trash home." Violet's words were quiet but the fury in each syllable echoed the shriek she'd let out.

"Mama, stop!"

"That's enough, Mama."

"Will, stop her!"

Will and his siblings all attempted to calm Violet. Will didn't even look at Debra. She didn't wait to see his reaction. She needed to get out of there.

What a mistake to think she could bring comfort to anyone, especially Will.

Present Day
Buffalo, New York
Debra

"I'M GOING TO HAVE to stay here tonight, babe."

"I know. I don't want you to even try to come home, do you hear me, Will?" I muted the volume of the television that perched on our kitchen counter. Images of whiteouts and cars with barely discernible headlights filled the screen.

Will laughed. "I couldn't if I wanted to. The police department just sent out a mass e-mail to all the business owners. It's an offense to go out except in an emergency—they're telling us all to stay put."

"It's supposed to last through tomorrow. You have enough in the pantry?" I smiled into the receiver. *Pantry* wasn't the appropriate word. Will owned an office in a business high-rise that had every possible amenity needed by today's businessperson on-site. Yoga studio, gym, pool, three different eating areas, a small movie theater. The various companies could continue to function even when the weather locked them in for an indefinite length of time.

"They're getting ready to serve chili tonight."

"I wish I was there to join you."

"No, you don't." We both laughed as he called my bluff.

"Okay, so I like being at home and having my work nearby. Sue me."

"Is Angie safe at her apartment or is she bunking in at the weather station?"

"This morning she told me she was going back to her place for some things, then back to work for the duration. I don't think it'll be much fun for her, even with her morning sickness easing up."

"At least she isn't out on the road."

"No. She was supposed to call me when she got to her place but I imagine she's back at work. I'll call her on her cell in a bit."

"She's fine, Deb."

Silence draped comfortably across the miles of phone line. I knew Will wanted to continue the conversation as much as I did, but since we weren't in the same room it was difficult.

"I'm going to get some work done before dinner," he said. "I'll call you later."

"Okay. Bye for now." I hung up and looked at Rose.

"Time to go get Violet, sweet dog." After breakfast I'd walked Vi back to her cottage to get more things for her overnight stay with us. I needed to bring her back to the house before the snow made it too difficult for her to walk.

Rose's tail thumped on the plush cream carpet. She loved going out in the snow, even if it was only for a short walk to Violet's cottage.

Before I could get my outer clothes on, the doorbell rang. Violet. I thought it was odd that she'd walked around the house instead of just to the kitchen door. Was the snow blowing that fiercely despite the protection of the tall pine trees?

I yanked open the front door and gasped in surprise. "Angie!"

"Hey, Mom."

Angie hurried in, her face visible through a tiny space between her snow-covered scarf and hood.

"Wow, what did you do, walk from the station?"

My question was purely rhetorical, since the weather station was on the other side of town, near the airport.

"No, just from my car. Which, thank God, is a four-wheel drive."

"I thought you were going back to work and staying there?" My stomach began to jump. What was Angie thinking, driving through a blizzard—especially now that she was pregnant?

"I was, but I got delayed leaving the station. I didn't expect it to be a problem, though. This wasn't supposed to pick up until later, around seven."

"You know better than anyone how quickly the weather can change in Buffalo. Have you forgotten?"

"I guess I have. The radar picture looked great when I left work, and I was sure I had a minimum of two hours to get home and back." The trip usually took her twenty minutes each way. "But I didn't count on all the traffic from the folks leaving work or the slow school busses from early dismissal."

"The news said they let the kids out at noon."

"Yes, and at three-thirty some of them still weren't home. The bus drivers will probably be stuck in the depot."

"So why are you here? I mean, I'm glad you are, but weren't you concerned about driving in this?"

"I figured that if I have to be stuck during a storm and it can't be at work, I want to be with you. Besides, my cupboards are bare and I need to eat when I can handle it."

I remembered my own pregnancies. The nausea ran my life the first three months, both times.

"The phone and Internet are still on, so you should be able to get some work done if you need to. I'm on my way to get Violet."

"She won't come over if she still has power and heat."

"You're right, but I'll drag her back with me. Once she finds out you're here, she'll come over in a flash."

"Let me go get her, Mom."

"You want to? Okay, that would be great." I put my coat back on its hook. "I'll make a pot of tea and throw something in the oven for dinner."

"Be right back."

Angie flounced through the foyer and into the kitchen, dripping all the way. Rose chased after her, tail wagging.

"Take Rose with you!"

"Okay."

The sound of the wind rose as Angie opened the kitchen door and then it slammed shut. I stared at the puddles of melted snow Angie had left. I supposed I should begin cleaning up the mess but at the moment all I felt was gratitude that my family was safe.

I needed to check in on the boys. As I went to the phone I caught my reflection in the sliding-glass door window. Wearing my hand-knit brown alpaca sweater and with my hair in corkscrews, I looked like a grizzly bear.

I laughed. I was still Mama bear, despite what Will had said. I wouldn't be happy until I knew all my cubs were safe. No matter what their age.

CHAPTER SIXTEEN

Present Day
Buffalo, New York
Debra

AN HOUR LATER, Angie brought Violet back, complete with an overnight case. I'd just hung up with Brian, having discovered that it was sunny and clear in Colorado.

"Violet, you live across the yard, not the Atlantic." I eyed the bulging duffel.

"There's a lot more needed to keep me running these days."

Violet replied to me but smiled at Angie. She'd always had a soft spot for Angie and all her grandchildren. In many ways, the children had allowed for the healing that needed to take place between Will, Violet and me.

"I'll take your bag upstairs, Vi. You sit down and get comfortable." Violet looked at the table, which I'd set with teacups and a plate of homemade cookies.

"You shouldn't go to so much trouble. It's just us."

I didn't respond as I carried Violet's bag to the back bedroom. Originally intended as our master suite, we'd redesigned it as a guest room when it was clear Violet would be living with us. Her arthritis made climbing stairs difficult at best.

Violet never accepted any of my gestures of hospitality without a fuss. To Violet, doing more than absolutely necessary was frivolous—and suspect.

I doubted that would ever change.

Will's siblings had relied on Violet and, of course, Dr. Bradley's money for far too long. Violet had to know they used her and got in touch only when they needed her. Neither Will's brother nor sister ever volunteered to take care of her. They never even checked up on her. Just her bank account.

When I came back to the kitchen I found Angie and Violet at the table, laughing.

"What's so funny?"

Angie's eyes sparkled with mirth.

"Grandma was telling me about the time Daddy played with his father's medical tools in the sandbox."

A smile teased the corners of my mouth. I'd heard the story from Will more than once. Since Will was interested in construction and building, even at age five, it made sense that he'd be interested in anything mechanical.

Problem was, the tool Will picked to hoist his mud bricks was a speculum, used for gynecological exams. Violet had been horrified but Will's dad had just laughed and said, "The boy knows what he needs to get the job done."

The fact that Violet was reiterating this to Angie intrigued me. Violet really saw her legacy in my daughter.

"Let me brown some meat and get a stew going. Does that sound good?"

"Order out. You sit." Violet had never cooked and didn't understand my love of the kitchen.

"Sure, and they'll deliver it on a snowmobile," I muttered under my breath as I pulled out my favorite Dutch oven and some onions. Violet's and Angie's voices rose and fell in the rhythm of familiar conversation.

Another blizzard.

How many had I survived in Buffalo?

AFTER OUR TEA I left Vi and Angie to their girl chat and went back to my fiber studio.

I delved into the second of the three huge cedar chests that housed my hand-knit work. I'd knitted through many if not all of the Buffalo storms I'd lived through. There was no better way to pass the time, even if it meant knitting by candlelight.

I found the tissue-wrapped items I sought—various small pieces of clothing, mostly winter scarves and hats. Could I recall the year for each? And with a little Internet help, match them up to specific blizzards?

I felt my excitement rise. It was getting too close to the exhibit to totally switch gears, but I could find a whole new theme for the show in these chests. Snowstorms could serve as a backdrop for my work.

I reached in and pulled out a half-done woman's vest. It was an argyle design I'd taken from a sock pattern and hoped to translate to this particular vest, in forest green, orange and brown. But I'd never finished it.

I'd started the vest right after I returned to Boston in 1973. The reason I'd stopped was downstairs talking to Vi. No way could I wear that vest with my growing belly. We didn't bare our bellies in the seventies, no matter how artsy or hippy we were.

That had been a hard, lonely time for me, but it had been worth it.

My thoughts raced back to the night Angie was conceived. That had been another tough time. But our lovemaking had been symbolic of the connection that kept us going.

August 1973
Crystal Beach, Ontario, Canada

AS IT BLEW THROUGH the car window, the hot wind cooled the nape of her neck. Debra had managed to borrow her mother's car for the night, because Linda's friend was taking her to bingo. Debra had promised she'd meet Will near Crystal Beach.

They'd barely seen each other since the funeral. The few times they'd gone out, Will was quiet and less affectionate than usual.

She knew he needed a chance to grieve his father's death. But she still hadn't been able to shake the sense of betrayal she'd felt when Will told her they needed to delay their wedding.

Debra didn't mind waiting as far as the actual ceremony was concerned. She needed the year to finish her degrees, and Will needed time to wind up his father's business and to start his own. He was right on those accounts.

She pulled up to the customs booth.

"What is your destination?" the uniformed woman asked.

"Crystal Beach."

"For how long?"

"Just the night."

"Citizenship?"

"U.S."

"Have a nice visit."

Debra pulled away, resenting that she and Will hadn't driven up here together. Canadian Customs probably wouldn't care that they were black and white but coming back over could be a problem. It was a few years ago but many people hadn't forgotten the racial incident on the ferry between Crystal Beach and Buffalo.

She let the air that blew through the car windows soothe her. Going to the cottage alone was a small price to pay to be with Will.

He was waiting for her at the cottage. His parents had purchased it years ago, but Will had told her they hadn't used it much recently. His dad was always working, and with his siblings out of the house, his parents just didn't take the time to come up here.

Will was standing in the drive. She could make out the lighted cottage, farther up the gravel road behind him.

She leaned her head out the window. "Where should I park?"

"Over there's fine." He pointed to a clear area under a grove of pine trees.

Even though they were at Crystal Beach, the actual lakefront was almost a mile up the road. This cottage was one of a group of three, and she saw that the other two cottages were full of weekenders.

Her hands shook as she turned off the ignition. She

had the horrible realization that she had no control over what Will was going to say.

They needed to talk; that much was certain. They'd avoided each other for the past three weeks. They'd been the loneliest weeks of Debra's life, but she'd busied herself with work at the restaurant and preparing to go back to Boston for her final year of school.

"Deb." Will's husky voice caressed her skin through the humid evening air.

She got out of the driver's seat and closed the door.

"Hi." She hated how high and tinny her voice sounded. She didn't need Will Bradley's pity, nor his compassion. She needed *him*.

"Come on in." He waited for her to walk ahead of him. He didn't ask if she had a bag. She did, but didn't want to admit it. Not unless this night changed the situation between them.

The cottage was as hot as the air outside, but the dim lighting made it seem cooler. Citronella candles flickered on the porch steps and she saw a few inside. Debra liked how the flames flickered against the orange and green glass holders. It reminded her of happier summers with Will.

"What about your mother?"

"She doesn't know we're here and doesn't need to. She's at home with my sister. She thinks I'm in New York."

"Oh." So he'd lied to spend this time with her.

Why did this surprise her? He hadn't wanted to stand up to his family about their engagement, and of course, how could she object now, when Dr. Bradley had died over this whole mess?

Will walked up to her and stroked her cheek. She let him, then immediately hated herself. She took a wide step backward.

"You look so sad, Deb."

"Why did you want me to meet you here, Will?"

"We need to talk. You know that."

She stole a glance at his face. His brown eyes reflected the candlelight and showed his sorrow of the past weeks. But in the depths of those eyes she saw what she'd always known—Will's desire for her.

She looked away.

"Can we sit down?"

Debra felt awkward as she moved to a tiny kitchen area and sat at an equally small table. Will took the chair opposite hers. She felt his body heat radiate across the foot or so of space.

"I don't feel right being here. This is your family's place, Will."

"My brother and sister both know I'm here with you. They don't have a problem with it."

"But your mother—"

"No more talk about my mother. Not tonight." Will's lips were pursed. She took a closer look at his face. She knew it so well, yet it seemed new to her. There were fresh lines at the creases of his eyes, and his forehead was lined, too. It was as though he'd aged a decade in three weeks.

"How are you *really* doing with your dad being gone, Will?"

Will broke eye contact with her and gazed over her shoulder.

"I'm okay. It's still not real to me, but then again, I have to take care of all the paperwork, the business closure, all of it. That brings it home."

Debra remained silent.

"You know he liked you, don't you, Deb? He was never into appearances like Mama is. He wanted each of us kids to be happy, and he provided us with the means to go after our dreams. As long as they were college dreams."

Will's chuckle rumbled through the cottage.

"He wasn't keen on Jimmy going to West Point, but I know he would've been proud to see Jimmy at the funeral in his cadet full dress grays."

"He did look handsome." Debra had seen Jimmy but was unable to talk to him because of the commotion caused by her visit.

Will turned his focus completely back to her.

"Deb, I owe you so much. I should've come to you sooner, but I couldn't."

"Will, stop! You owe me nothing. Not anymore."

"What do you mean, not anymore?"

"It's not going to work, is it? This is just too hard on you, your family. My family's not thrilled, either." She said the words she'd practiced as she'd crossed the Peace Bridge.

"Deb, Deb. There's no way this *can't* work." He reached across the table and grasped her hands.

She loved how his large dark hands enfolded her small pale ones. As though he could protect her from anything. But now she had to protect him from himself.

She shook her head. "No, Will. You deserve to have a life as free and glorious as your father wanted for you. It won't happen with me. They'll always be talking about you, and not because you're a great architect. You want the professionals you'll be dealing with to see you as an equal. They won't if you're married to a white woman."

"I thought color didn't matter to you."

"It doesn't matter to *me*, Will. It matters to everyone else, most folks out there. And because of that, it should matter to you."

"You're the last person who should be telling me that." His look was unbelieving, almost one of shock.

"I know you best, don't I?"

"I thought you did. But apparently we haven't been communicating as well as I'd perceived."

"Will, I love you too much to let this ruin you."

Will stood up and pulled her to her feet. His arm encircled her waist while his other hand slipped under her hair.

Shivers ran down her skin. His eyes reflected intense desire—desire she'd seen a glimpse of in the Paris apartment. This was the real Will. Raw, virile, undeterred.

The man she loved. This came to her in a jolt, just as his lips touched hers.

Will was an expert at kissing her. He always cajoled the deepest response from her with his persuasive whispers, strokes and caresses. He knew just where to place his lips to elicit tremors of desire. Debra often laughed at how the simple act of holding Will's hand made her feel steamy inside.

They shared a real chemistry, all right.

But this kiss wasn't a seduction. And it wasn't just chemistry. Will claimed her with this kiss. He convinced her that they belonged together.

He pulled back an inch, and Debra moaned.

"Don't stop now, Will."

"Open your eyes, Deb."

She did, and looked up into his. The pupils were dilated in the dim light and made her want him all the more.

"Come over here. Sit down." He eased them both onto the couch.

"Don't you get it, babe? It doesn't matter to me what anyone else thinks. Yeah, I know it won't be easy—it sure hasn't been so far. But I love you. And the pain I'll carry the rest of my life, the *regret,* over losing you— it's more than any man could handle. More than I ever want to handle."

"Oh, Will." She didn't disagree with him. But she also knew that she didn't want him to look at her twenty years down the road and see all the opportunities he'd missed.

His hands were moving up and down her rib cage, her hips. When they moved down to her bottom she forgot about her resolve to do only "what's best for Will."

His kisses grew more insistent and the couch more cramped.

"Let me make love to you the right way, Deb." His breath felt warm against her cheek.

"Yes."

Debra couldn't muster the strength to fight Will, nor

did she want to deny herself this pleasure. They'd always shared a love that had grown, matured, while they were in Paris.

They kissed for a few more minutes until Debra ached with the need to have Will inside of her.

"Will, wait."

She pushed him back and made herself stand up.

"Let me get my blanket out of the car—we can spread it out here."

His eyes were full of desire and anticipation.

"Hurry."

Debra did just that. Once she got outside, the night closed in on her. She reached for the car's door handle and paused. She had the keys, and her purse was still on the seat. She could get in the car and leave now, before they intensified their relationship even more.

Would it make leaving Will any easier?

She knew what she had to do. It was the only way to save Will's chance at a successful life.

But she wanted him now, at this moment, tonight.

Debra yanked open the car door and grabbed the blanket they'd made love on many times in Paris. It was a scrap blanket she'd knitted from whatever leftover yarn she'd had or could find at the French *brocantes* or flea markets. She loved the colors—lots of pale blues, with splashes of red and gold.

It was *their* blanket. Until they had a home of their own one day, a bed of their own.

It'll never happen.

Debra shoved the thought down and headed back inside the cottage.

Will was waiting for her, his shirt and jeans off, in his briefs. The sight of him standing in the tiny cottage sitting room made all their problems fade away. Just for tonight...

They deserved one last time together, didn't they?

CHAPTER SEVENTEEN

Present Day
Buffalo, New York

ANGIE WALKED into the spare room that served as her parents' second guest room. She was about to toss her overnight bag onto the bed but stopped when she saw that it wasn't empty.

Piles of sweaters, afghans, socks, hats and mittens lay strewn atop the burgundy satin comforter. Angie let the shoulder strap slide down and dropped her bag next to her feet. She moved toward the bed, her fingers itching to feel all the things her mother had made over the years.

Looking through Debra's knitting was like looking through Grandma Violet's jewelry chest. No hint of perfume wafted from them, though. Instead she smelled a distinct aroma of cedar and lavender. Cedar from the storage chest and lavender from the special soap Debra used to clean and preserve her treasures.

Angie pulled out a bright, multicolored vest she remembered wearing in elementary school. The colors screamed early eighties, but the style was one that had returned.

The vest was special to Angie. She'd won the city-wide spelling bee in it when she was in fifth grade. She'd insisted on wearing it each and every time she had to compete, which meant Debra had to wash out lunch-room ketchup and chocolate pudding more than once. This was evident in the pilling and overall fuzziness of the sweater.

"You found my stash. I forgot I'd pulled all of this out." Debra came into the room and gave Angie a quick hug.

"Mom, remember this vest?"

Debra laughed. "How could I forget it? You all but slept in it."

"It's a magic vest."

"Until you turned on it." Debra referred to the day Angie finally lost the round of spelling bees she was assigned to, at the county level.

"Hey, *it* turned on *me*. It didn't like being washed so often."

Debra just smiled.

"Why did you take all this stuff out now, Mom?"

Debra didn't answer right away. She ran her hands over the pile closest to her, studying the baby kimono she'd made Angie after they'd moved back to Buffalo.

"I'm looking for ideas for what to make the new baby. And any future babies."

"Mom." Angie knew her tone got her message across from the way Debra folded her arms.

"A mother can look at her things, can't she?"

"Mom, you've been edgy for the past couple of days. What's going on?"

Debra fingered the edge of a blue baby bonnet.

"Your father seems to think I feel some kind of guilt over any problems you and your brothers have gone through. He says I believe it's because of our marriage."

"Do you?" Angie wanted to hear if her mother really did believe that.

"What mother doesn't feel responsible for her children's lives?"

"When the kids are young, sure, but Mom, we're all adults. Tell me one thing that's wrong with any of us because we have a white mother and a black father."

"I'm not talking about external issues, Angie. You all have excellent educations and are all successful in your chosen professions."

"So your point is?"

Debra sighed.

Heat crawled up Angie's neck. "Mom, I sense an incredible amount of judgment in that sigh. First, I'm not a weak woman who needs a man to rescue me. I have enough confidence in myself to know I'm okay just the way I am. And I happened to fall in love with a man who isn't baby-crazy—there are worse things."

Silence crept into the room.

"I'm sorry, Angie. But you can't blame me for worrying about you. Especially now that you're pregnant."

"I thought you'd be happy to be a grandmother."

"I am, honey, I just want *you* to be happy. And I know from experience that being a single parent isn't any fun."

"Grandma Linda is from a different generation. It's acceptable to raise a child alone now. I'm prepared to do it if I have to."

"I don't think you'll have to worry about that, do you, sweetheart? Jesse will catch his breath and be thrilled when it all settles out."

Angie wasn't in a mood to argue with her mother. Plus, a huge part of her hoped Debra was right.

Half an hour later, the ring of her cell phone brought Angie out of her thoughts, which were still on the conversation with her mother. She didn't recognize the number on caller ID.

"Hello?"

"Angie? Sweetie?"

Jesse. His voice washed over her like a hot bath, and she luxuriated in the sensuous feel of it.

"Ange, are you there?" His voice was more tense, almost frantic.

"I'm here."

His laughter lifted her heart.

"Listen, Ange, I only have ten minutes."

"Okay." She needed at least ten minutes to get over her shock.

"It's good to hear your voice." Jesse's declaration so early in their conversation caught Angie off guard.

"Angie?"

"I'm here," she said again.

"I've tried to call you at the apartment but you must be at the weather station a lot."

"I'm surprised you were able to get through on my cell."

Jesse's laugh rippled across thousands of miles of satellite linkups.

"Thank God for modern technology."

Thank God I didn't change my cell-phone number yet.

"I know what you mean," she said.

Angie realized that her voice, her replies, were stilted. But she couldn't bring herself to say more. She was so relieved to hear Jesse's voice—but she was afraid of saying too much.

"What's going on? Are you excited about the storm? I saw it on CNN."

Sure enough, Jesse sensed she was off-kilter, and not just because of their rift.

"Yeah, I'm psyched about it."

Liar, liar. I'm stuck in the last place I wanted to be during my first Buffalo storm.

"Have you read my e-mails?"

"Of course."

"How come you haven't replied?"

"It's…hard to put my feelings in an e-mail."

"That's all we've got right now, Ange."

"It doesn't come easy to me, Jesse."

His use of the endearment wasn't lost on her.

"I'm lucky to grab twenty or thirty minutes to myself every day. I've never done so many surgeries, one on top of the other."

"You sound happy about it."

"Yeah, I am. To know I've had a part in saving even one of these young troops is an incredible rush."

"What about when you can't do anything?"

"We try to, anyhow, and know that we gave it our best."

Angie's love for Jesse swelled in a wave of longing.

This was the man she'd fallen in love with. The man passionate about life.

Not the man who refused to consider a baby or family.

"Ange?"

"Hmm?"

"I want to open up our discussion about a family."

It wasn't the first time he'd practically read her mind. Angie stared at the wallpaper in the room that had been hers as a teenager.

"Maybe we should stay away from that, Jesse," she finally said. "It never ends well." And she couldn't take the rejection. Not now. The pregnancy had just started to seem real to her.

"Angie, I'm not saying I've had a complete change of heart, but maybe we should put the idea of having kids back on the table."

"Wh-what?"

Jesse had never even breathed the word *kid* as a possibility in any of their conversations. It had never *been* on the table.

"Being over here has made me rethink some things. We have an awful lot to offer a child."

Glad you've figured that out.

"Are you there?"

"Yes. Look, Jesse, you're right. We need to talk. But not now, not like this. I'm at Mom and Dad's, and as you know, there's a major blizzard bearing down on us. I can't even get back to the weather station. Grandma Vi is here, and I can't focus on us. Not just now."

She could've added that her hormones had scrambled her brains but didn't.

"I have to go now anyway. But we're not done, Angie."

"Bye, Jesse."

"I love—"

His words were cut off with a sharp crackle. He'd exceeded his ten-minute limit.

"COME AND SIT BY ME, girl." Violet patted the red sofa cushion beside her.

"Hey, Grandma." Angie slid next to Violet and hugged her grandmother. Ever since she could remember, Angie had relied on Grandma Violet as a source of unconditional love and comfort.

"You doing okay, sweetie?" Violet squeezed Angie's thigh and peered at her through thick, round glasses.

"I'm fine, Grandma."

"Not by the look on your face. What's up? You and Jesse going to work things out or not?" Vi didn't know Angie was pregnant yet, but she sensed her angst over being apart from Jesse.

"I hope so, Grandma. But I've been wrong before."

"Do you love him?"

"Yes. But sometimes that's not enough."

"Baloney." Violet spat the word out, hands resting in her lap. Grandma Vi smelled as she always did, of lilac perfume and muscle ointment.

"Nowadays, you kids think too much. In my day you married the boy you loved and you stayed with him."

"Not everyone was as happy as you and Grandpa, Grandma Vi."

"No, they weren't."

Angie held her breath. She knew the circumstances of her grandfather's death and had never discussed them with Grandma. Even though Grandma and Mom had made amends years ago, it had to be a painful memory.

"You don't want regrets, Angie gal. The worst thing in life is regret. Mistakes, harsh words, thoughtless acts, they can all be forgiven, repaired. But a *regret*—" Violet shook her head "—you can't go back and redo it. If Jesse's the man for you, go after him. Love doesn't fall into our laps with no effort on our part, you know."

"Do you have regrets, Grandma?"

"Some. But this isn't about me."

Angie remained silent. She knew when to push with Grandma Vi and when to just sit still.

"What's your mama making for dinner?"

The aroma of stew curled into the living room, and Angie's stomach grumbled.

"Smells like beef stew. Maybe some homemade biscuits if we're lucky."

"See if we can eat here, in front of the TV."

"Sure thing, Grandma." Angie smiled as she stood up and walked past the fireplace, toward the kitchen. She had so many wonderful memories of this house. She remembered past storms with the entire family around the fire, drinking hot chocolate and praying school would be canceled.

This wasn't the worst place to be stranded, after all.

"You have the remote, Grandma?"

"Yes, right here. I'm going to see what's on the talk shows."

CHAPTER EIGHTEEN

Present Day
Buffalo, New York
Debra

"HEY, MOM."

"Hey." I looked up from the cake batter I was spooning into a bundt pan. "Who was on the phone? Work?"

"No. Jesse."

I bit my tongue to keep from saying anything. Will's challenge to me to stay out of Angie's life was proving more difficult as each snowflake fell.

"Mom, you don't have to look so strained."

"I'm not strained. I just respect your privacy."

Angie rolled her eyes; I ignored it. "Since when?" she asked.

"Since I have my own life." I glanced at the oven as it beeped that the temperature was ready for baking.

"Jesse wants to talk about having kids."

"And you don't?"

Angie played with the wooden utensils I kept in an old crockery pot on the granite counter. The cracked pot was incongruous with the sleek counter, but it had caught my eye at a local antique show.

"I do want to talk to him. But I don't think I can handle his reaction when he finds out I'm pregnant."

"Oh, Angie." I bit my lip—again. At this rate it was going to start bleeding. Damn.

I refused to say anything. Even though I was convinced it would be best if she simply told him and let him adjust to the idea.

"Mom, what was that about not judging?"

"I'm not judging, Angie. I just hate to see you repeat my mistakes." Surely the pain I'd put myself through all those years ago had to be worth something?

"I'll tell him. But I want to do it in person." I knew why. She wanted to see his expression of joy and love for her, for the baby. But Angie's going to Iraq was not an option.

"That's impossible, isn't it?"

"Probably. But Jesse did mention in one of his e-mails that he gets an R & R, rest and relaxation, for a week in the middle of his detachment there."

"Which is?"

"Next month."

"He'd come here?"

"He could, but then we'd only have four days together. Since he'll have been there less than three months, he won't be allowed too much time off. We'd have more time if I went to meet him."

"Where? Surely you wouldn't go to Iraq?"

"No, no, I can meet him at the Armed Forces Recreation Center in Germany. It's in the Bavarian Alps and sounds wonderful. Jesse said I could look it up online."

"As long as you think your health can handle it."

I worried about her even though I knew she was in no danger. But a long flight, a foreign country—it didn't feel as cozy a place for my pregnant daughter as I'd like it to.

ANGIE WATCHED in bemusement as Debra stirred the stew, tasted from her ancient wooden spoon, then opened three more bottles of herbs and spices. Her mother's movements were deliberate as she added various flavors to the stew, one shake here, two there. Angie had never tired of watching her mother cook.

"What?"

Debra looked up from her near-meditative task and smiled at Angie.

"Nothing. I just like watching you. You're amazing, Mom." Angie was grateful her nausea abated in the late afternoons so she could appreciate all the heavenly scents coming from Debra's pots.

"I am, aren't I?" Debra laughed, the sound low as it echoed around the great room. Violet's poor hearing even picked it up.

"What's funny about that?" Angie and Debra looked over at the television screen. Violet was watching the latest celebrity news, dealing with a famous divorce and the prospective child-custody case. She had the closed captioning activated, so the volume wasn't as loud as she kept it in her own home.

"Nothing, Grandma."

Angie went back to sit on the sofa, beside Violet. She grabbed one of the many hand-knit throws Debra had made over the years and wrapped it around herself, not unlike Violet, who sat with her shawl on her shoulders and a blanket over her legs. The fire crackled and kept the room warm, but with the snow pelting the windows and the howling of the wind, it was hard not to feel chilled.

Angie called to Debra.

"Mom, come on out here for a while before we lose the cable. You've been working and cooking all day."

"I'm coming." Angie knew that tone of voice—her mother could keep puttering all night. Usually Daddy got her out of her working frenzies, but he was stuck in his office.

"*Now,* Mom." Angie found it ironic that she was about to become a mother herself, yet yearned for Debra's comfort and closeness more than ever.

Her head told her it was just the changes in her body that were making her feel more sentimental. But the all-too-frequent lumps in her throat, her trembling lips, the tears that splattered on her cheeks—these were from her heart, from the center of what she knew herself to be.

And all of that started with Debra.

With her mother.

After Debra put the burner on low and set the timer, she came into the family room and settled next to Angie on the sofa. Angie held up a portion of her blanket to share.

"Thanks, honey." They snuggled beside each other as they'd always done.

Relieved that her mother was finally relaxing, Angie shifted her gaze back to her grandmother.

Vi sat on the leather chair, her feet on the matching ottoman. Her attention was on the television with the incessant drone of the celebrity anchorwoman's reporting. Who had cuddled Vi as a child?

Grandma Violet never spoke of her family. She said her life started when she met Benjamin Bradley, the grandfather Angie had never known. From the snippets Angie and her brothers had put together over the years, they'd learned that Vi's family had moved from the South in the late nineteenth century. Vi was the great-great-great-granddaughter of slaves.

They were Angie's ancestors, too. As a teenager, but especially as a college student, Angie had spent hours wondering about her divided family tree—the enslaved African-American side, on which her grandmother and father stood and made their own success, and the Polish-American side that still struggled in their day-to-day blue-collar jobs. Sometimes both parents working two jobs still couldn't pay all the bills, let alone college expenses. Her maternal grandmother had found her own version of happiness with Mom's stepfather, but had never formed a close bond with Debra, Will or their children.

With a start Angie realized she wanted more for her baby. She wanted a family just like the one Debra and Will had made.

ANGIE HESITATED before she hit the enter button. Once she did, she'd be committed to the tickets. She'd be going to meet Jesse in Europe.

Her nausea remained ever-present, but she hoped it would begin to dissipate within the next few weeks. She was finally finishing the first trimester.

"Okay, why not?" She hit the button, and went on to her e-mail.

Three messages from Jesse in the past hour.

The clock on her computer registered 12:30 a.m. That meant it was near breakfast time for Jesse.

Anwar province, Iraq
Hi, baby,
Early day today. Just wrapped up after two tough surgeries. I'll go right back after I send this and grab something to eat. One thing for sure, I'm not putting on any weight here. No chance to sit and eat a regular meal. The food looks great, and the mess workers really outdo themselves, but even one day without new casualties is nonexistent. The troops are taking heavy hits out in the fire zone.

The e-mail ended without a closing comment, so Angie went to the next in the list.

Hi, Angie,
Saw the news. Buffalo looks like it's getting clobbered. I'm relieved to hear that you're at your folks' house. Sorry you're not at work, where you want to be right now. But at least you're not stuck on the road or worse. Those storms up there are harsh. Remember the one a few years ago?
Love,
Jesse

Yes, Angie remembered the storm. She and Jesse had flown in for Blair and Stella's wedding. It was early October, so they weren't expecting bad weather, and had found themselves stranded on the Thruway for three hours. They'd made good use of the time in the car, making out like teenagers. She knew it could've been worse.

She sighed and rubbed her belly. It wasn't much larger yet, but her body felt entirely different to her.

Jesse had always made it clear that he didn't want to risk having kids in light of his childhood. His own parents had each married three times, twice to each other. They were back together now, and had been for the past five years, but their divorces and respective marriages to other spouses had occurred during Jesse's junior and senior years in high school.

He'd never forgiven them.

Angie didn't blame him, but she did think he'd let his own resentment cloud his better judgment.

Angie and Jesse had been married for seven years, most of the time very content and happy. But Angie wanted kids. Jesse still balked at the idea, although she felt his reasons weren't entirely valid anymore. Yes, science supported the theory that an addiction gene existed and they'd always have a chance of passing it on to their offspring. But his nieces and nephews were living proof that environment played a huge part, too.

Angie never apologized for wanting children with Jesse. They just didn't address it.

Until his most recent phone call.

Her cell phone rang. The noise startled her in the still of the late hour.

It was Jesse again. Using today's ten minutes, in the first hour of his day in Iraq.

"Hi, Angie. How about meeting me in Paris instead of Garmisch?"

"Paris?" Angie's planning had revolved around Germany.

"Why not? It's warmer than the Alps and you've always wanted to go."

"I just booked a flight for Germany. I'm also new at my job, Jesse. I can't just take off whenever I want to. Especially during our busy season."

"It'll be the same week you've already booked off for vacation. Besides, every season's busy up there, isn't it? They have blizzards in October, for heaven's sake. Tell them you'll do overtime on Halloween."

Angie choked back a laugh. She'd have a two-month-old baby by Halloween.

Jesse's baby.

"It's not that easy."

"Do you think doing neurosurgery in a war zone is?"

Recrimination sent a flush of shame up her chest, her face.

Even pregnant and in the middle of a Buffalo blizzard, Angie knew she was far more secure and comfortable than Jesse, given where he was.

"I'll see what I can do." Was she crazy? It was as though her tongue had a mind of its own.

Debra

I STARED AT THE BOOKMARKS I'd cross-stitched for Will and me back in high school. Just another way I tried to be close to him. I couldn't have him as a normal boyfriend, but I never wanted him to forget me.

It's impossible to laugh at that girl, even now, over forty years later. Because the love I had then was the start of what we had now, what sustained us over the years.

"Mom?"

Angie interrupted my thoughts. I looked up from the studio desk.

"Yes, honey?"

"Grandma's settled in for the night. How long do you think you'll be up?"

I glanced at the clock. It was after 1:00 a.m.

"I had no idea it was so late. What are you doing up?" I studied her more closely. She looked tired but otherwise okay.

"Jesse just e-mailed, and then we talked on my cell phone for a bit."

"Okay." I wouldn't ask her to tell me any more than she was ready to. Will's warning had hit home. Angie was entitled to her own life.

She walked into the room.

"He wants me to meet him in Europe."

"You were expecting that, right? Didn't you say it would be at that resort in the Alps?" I was so proud of myself—I hadn't even mentioned that skiing wouldn't be an option for a pregnant woman.

"Yes, well, that's what he said at first, and I assumed it would be Germany, since that's where most of his colleagues have met their wives."

"And now?"

"He suggested we go to Paris instead."

"Oh…"

Paris. It was responsible for Will and me finally getting together, for admitting our love to each other. Paris meant so much to us that we'd never gone back for fear it would be different. For fear of ruining our beautiful memories, besmirching them with present realities.

"Don't get all worked up, Mom. Paris isn't anything to Jesse and me but a meeting place."

"Do you really believe that, Angie?"

"Mom." Angie wouldn't make eye contact; she concentrated on the knitted items I'd laid out on the table.

"What are these for? Golf clubs?"

Angie held up the burgundy covers that, unknown to her, might as well have been a scarlet *A*.

"Yes. I never finished them." And never went through with the physical side of an emotional adultery, thank God. It had just been a fantasy, and an opportunity I'd passed on.

"Angie, listen to me. I'm well aware that you could raise this child by yourself if you want to. But if you think you'll come to regret not mending your relationship with Jesse, then you have to try."

"I know." She sighed. "But there's another thing, Mom. I'll miss your opening night of the exhibit."

"That's okay. It'll still be here when you get back." Of course I wanted Angie there for opening night, but I wanted her family situation settled more.

She held up the tiny ivory cardigan she'd worn to our wedding. She'd been all of six weeks old.

"You made this for me?"

"I did." I hesitated for just a moment. What the hell.

My grandchild wasn't coming into a family of secrets, not if I had anything to say about it. And I did.

"You know we didn't get married until after you were born, right?"

"Yes, you told me in the coffee shop." Angie frowned at me. "Did you intend to marry Daddy once you left Buffalo?"

"No. Yes, of course." I sighed. "I don't know what I thought. I knew I needed to finish my degree, and I knew that I couldn't come back until it was done."

I watched her finger the delicate baby sweater.

"Your dad was going through a difficult time that year with his dad, your grandfather, passing away, and well…Grandma wasn't always so easy to deal with."

"Mom, Grandma's never been easy to deal with. She and I have a bond, but don't think I haven't noticed her bossiness."

"Bossiness is one thing. How she was before…" I looked out at the snow that was blowing so hard it made a musical *pling-pling* against the windowpanes.

"I've told you and your brothers that times were different then, even as recently as twenty years ago. You've seen a huge change in your lifetime, haven't you?"

"You're back on the color issue, Mom. I'm telling you, it's never been the problem for me that you expected it to be."

"Angie, you've been blessed with beauty and smarts. For the most part you've always been around people as educated as you. And don't lie to me. I know you've had your own struggles."

I drew in a long breath, then exhaled.

"My point is that when your dad and I got married, we could've been exactly alike, except for the color of our skin, and it wouldn't have been good enough."

"I studied African-American history, Mom. I get the social issues."

"I know you do, intellectually, and on some level, in your heart. But living through them is another matter."

I smiled at my daughter.

"I wouldn't change anything, Angie. I love your father and he's the man who I'm supposed to be with. He always was. That's why I'm saying you need to go after Jesse and work things out if you honestly believe he's the man for you. He'll come around on the family issue—it sounds like he already has. He's more committed to you than almost any husband I've met. And once he knows about the baby…"

"That's just it. I don't want him to want a family merely because he has no choice."

I had to laugh.

Angie's brows drew together. She didn't understand that I wasn't laughing at her.

"Honey, I had the same thoughts when I was pregnant with you, and right before your dad and I tied the knot. It isn't something you can control anymore, Angie. You and the baby are a package deal."

"I don't like being anybody's 'deal.'"

"Don't be so obtuse, Angie. You know what I'm getting at."

Angie gnawed at her lower lip. Her dark curls fell against her café-au-lait skin and I was struck again by what a beautiful woman she'd become.

"I thought by the time I was thirty-five I'd have the world figured out." I saw a tear slip out of her eye and roll down her cheek.

I walked over to her and hugged her tight.

"Oh, baby, we never get it figured out. That's the hell of it all. But…it's also the fun part."

Angie pulled away and rubbed her cheeks.

"Damn these hormones," she muttered.

"They're a good thing. They mean your body's doing what it's supposed to."

"Were you this emotional with me and the twins?"

"Oh, yeah. Some days it was all I could do to keep my mouth shut so I wouldn't say something horrible to some poor, undeserving soul."

Angie giggled. "I bit my new employee's head off for using up the last of the copy paper. There were stacks and stacks of it in the cabinet right next to the machine, but it didn't matter. I did apologize," she added quickly.

"I'd expect no less." I smiled at her. "Are you going to be able to sleep?"

"Yes. I wish I was at the station, but this is the way it is. If they need me they can call me on my cell."

"It sounds like this storm will stop by noon tomorrow."

"Yes, that's what my systems are indicating. So I can get to the station then."

"Angie, you're forgetting one thing."

"What, Mom?"

"It'll take a day for the city to clear the streets. Just look out at that driveway. I'll bet there are three feet of snow. You're not going anywhere until it's safe."

"Something else I don't have any control over."

I remained silent. This was a precious hour Angie and I wouldn't normally get, between her career and mine. Our coffee-shop meetings were great but not the same. They didn't allow enough time for these heart-to-hearts.

Which on most days was fine with both of us.

But tonight we needed the connection.

I WOKE SUDDENLY in the middle of the dark night. The howl of the blizzard hadn't lessened, and the house continued to make its familiar groans. The storm hadn't awakened me, but my dreams had. They weren't so much dreams as thoughts that continued the conversation Angie and I had started last night.

I remembered the early years, how our marriage had begun....

CHAPTER NINETEEN

May 1974
Boston, Massachusetts

THE DOORBELL RANG right as Debra was changing the messiest diaper Angie had ever produced. She was only three weeks old and Debra breastfed her, so the poop didn't smell. But the mess had a way of oozing through every diaper edge possible.

"Mrs. Irwin, could you get the door for me?"

Debra smiled at her angel, poop or no poop. It was astonishing how a baby could soothe a broken heart, mend a shattered dream.

She finished changing Angie and smoothed out her own dress. It was graduation day. Mrs. Irwin had insisted Debra get her diploma in person. It was going to be a hot day again. With her swollen breasts and still-aching body, Debra didn't relish spending a couple of hours at the ceremony. But she'd be able to sit down and rest for a bit—that couldn't be bad, could it?

"Who was it?"

Debra walked into the tiny front sitting room, Angie perched on her shoulder.

"It's me, Deb."

Debra credited motherly instincts and unseen angels with the fact that she didn't drop Angie on the floor. Will stood off to the side of the foyer; she didn't know how she hadn't seen him at once. His height and muscular body made enough of a statement, but in his suit and tie, and with the spark of triumph in his eyes, he all but knocked Debra off her feet.

"Will!"

"I've found you." His gaze feasted on her as though he were starved for the sight of her. She saw him take in her face, her hair, skim her body. And rest on the back of Angie's head.

"I thought you were graduating today."

Debra watched the emotions play across his face. He was trying to figure out if she had a friend or relative visiting with a young baby.

"Today *is* graduation day. How did you know?"

"I called the school. I wanted to surprise you."

Instead, Debra thought, he'd surprised himself. At least, he was about to get the surprise of his life.

"Oh."

"You look tired." His voice sounded tentative. No doubt Mrs. Irwin's presence threw him off, too.

"Why don't I take Angie for a walk?" Mrs. Irwin reached out to Debra, but Debra's hand tightened on her slumbering child.

"Not right now, Mrs. Irwin. Would you mind, if, um…"

"Not at all, dear. I'll run and get the groceries you need and come back in time for you to leave."

"Thank you." Debra smiled her gratitude at the woman.

The screen door slammed shut behind Mrs. Irwin, and Debra and Will stood where they were, staring at one another.

"I've missed you, Debra."

"Let's sit down, Will."

The only place to sit was a tiny love seat Debra had brought from Buffalo last year.

Their immediate proximity stole her breath away and would soon rob her of rational thought. Maybe she should've suggested they take Angie for a walk.

"What's with the baby, Deb?" Will's voice, right next to her, stirred the coals that always glowed for him in her heart.

Just go ahead. Get it over with.

"She's ours, Will."

His hands stilled on his lap, and she felt his breath catch.

"Ours?"

"Crystal Beach." The night they'd made love as though they'd never see each other again.

"Apparently the Pill isn't as effective if you miss a day or two." With the stress of Dr. Bradley's death and her schedule at the restaurant, she'd forgotten a couple of times. Still, she hadn't thought it would be a problem.

"You never told me?"

"I couldn't, Will. Not yet. I planned to." She clasped Angie tighter to her shoulder. "Not like this, of course."

"But *when?* Are you coming back to Buffalo?"

"No. I have a good job here in Boston. I can care for us both. Will, I don't want you to worry, I'm not going to ask you for anything. I can raise Angie."

"Without me?"

"Will, when I left…"

"Things were horrible, Deb. But they've calmed down, and even if they hadn't, I've learned one thing this year. That I don't want to live without you." He shook his head as though clearing it. "You never said anything about this in our phone calls."

No, she hadn't. They'd agreed they needed some space, but also agreed to talk regularly. The phone calls had always been a week or two apart. She and Will both needed to hear each other's voices.

"How could I, Will? I don't want you to feel guilty— or obligated to marry me because of the baby. We already talked about why marriage is too hard for us." As she spoke, big tears squeezed out of her eyes and onto the baby blanket.

"No, Deb, *you* talked about why we couldn't marry. I've never agreed with you. I know it won't be an easy path for us, but it isn't easy for anyone. My career's going well enough that I can support us, so we won't have to deal with a lot of the problems."

"You mean cocoon us in a rich house somewhere."

Just like his mother had been cocooned while married to his father. Out of touch with the real world, living her fantasy of the life she'd been raised in and expected her children to carry on.

A plan that did not include her eldest, Will, marrying a white woman from a lower economic class.

"No." He didn't argue further, just denied her accusation.

"It's a girl?"

"Yes. Meet your daughter, Angie. Angie, meet your daddy."

His gaze was so tender, so wondrous.

Debra lowered Angie into his arms.

"Here. Support her head. Like this."

Will took the bundle and looked down into Angie's face. His daughter.

"She's beautiful."

"Yes, she is."

"How old is she?"

"Three weeks."

He looked up at Debra. "So you've been pregnant all this time?"

Debra laughed. "Since you saw me last."

"This is why you didn't come home at Christmas."

"Yes. Plus I needed to get my dissertation done before I got too big or in case the baby came early."

"You finished everything?"

"Yes." She said the word quietly. Studying and working her usual demanding schedule had been difficult while she'd had morning sickness, and then again right after the birth. But with the help of a few friends and Mrs. Irwin, she'd come through.

Mrs. Irwin had been her landlady in graduate off-campus housing, but turned into a wonderful mentor when the baby came. And she loved helping out with Angie.

"You're not angry?"

Will kept staring at Angie, and held her tiny fingers in his.

"I am, and I will be, more so as I think about everything you've been through alone. But right now, Deb, I'm a daddy. We have a daughter."

Present Day
Buffalo, New York
Debra

I SMILED TO MYSELF. The dark-blue gloves I'd worn ragged in Paris still had their shape, despite the nearly four decades since I'd first cast on the yarn to make them. Memories of Paris and Will were never sad. I'd been able to let go of whatever fears and reluctance I'd had about our relationship and just *live*.

And love.

The phone rang. I grabbed it from the bedside table, holding the gloves in my right hand.

"Hello."

"Hi, babe." Will's sweet voice warmed my insides.

"Hi, honey. I miss you."

"Yeah, me, too. And I miss our bed. This couch is warm but my back's killing me."

"It doesn't look like you're coming home today." I glanced over at Will's side of the bed and sighed.

"Not until they get the major roads cleared."

"I just saw the news. The snow hasn't stopped and now they're saying it won't till later this evening."

"So if we're lucky maybe we'll be together tomorrow night."

"I hope so." I didn't think it would happen that quickly, even with Buffalo's advanced snow-removal equipment. But I didn't want Will to say I was being negative.

"What have you been doing?"

"Hanging out with Vi and Angie. Angie's still asleep. We were up late last night, talking."

"Oh?"

"I told her about our first year."

"Oh." His voice was flat. "What did she say?"

"Not much. She was a bit surprised, but when she thought about the times, she understood."

"Why tell her now? None of the kids ever asked about it before."

"Why should they? We were married before Angie was a year old, and of course the boys don't know any different."

"You haven't answered my question." I heard the tiredness in his voice from sleeping on the office couch. I also heard his defensiveness. He never wanted the kids, especially Angie, to ever think he was anything less than one hundred percent behind them.

"It's because she's pregnant, alone and trying to figure out how to tell Jesse."

"So you volunteered our circumstances from over thirty years ago?"

"It came up because of the sweater chests. I was pulling out some baby clothes to see what was still fit to wear. One thing led to another."

I didn't mention that I was changing the scope of my exhibit, or that I wasn't looking at my stash just for the new baby. I wasn't ready to tell him, not yet. Our argument was too fresh, and he'd think I was trying to pander to his arguments.

Will didn't reply, and I felt a hot rush of anger. Our story wasn't just Will's to tell or not tell. It was mine, too.

"Don't worry, Will, I didn't apologize for falling in love with a black man. And believe it or not, our conversation didn't have anything to do with you. I was the one raising Angie those first weeks, the one who birthed her and clothed her and provided for us both."

"Damn it, Debra, that was your choice!"

"Was it really my choice?" I heard his breath over the phone and mine was just as tense. There was a silence, as if neither of us dared speak.

"I don't think so, Will," I said eventually. "You needed time away from me at that point. If I'd come back to Buffalo at Christmas pregnant with your baby, God knows what would've happened. Your family needed time to heal from your dad's death."

We both knew what I meant—that Vi had needed time. She'd teetered on the brink of insanity in the aftermath of her beloved husband's early demise. My pregnancy, caused by her son, would have sent her over that brink.

"I never intended to keep Angie from you, Will. Not forever."

"I don't know, Deb."

An icy finger cooled my anger while stirring long-buried fears.

"What are you saying?"

"You were pretty comfortable when I showed up. You had a job, a wonderful babysitter and a nice home, for a graduate student. Is there any reason I should believe you would've told me about Angie any sooner?"

"Why are we having this conversation thirty-five years after the fact? You never mentioned any of this before, never questioned my motives for keeping Angie away from Buffalo in the beginning."

"I was younger. I was so damned relieved to have found you that I didn't care."

"Why care now?"

"The same reason you're rethinking us, Deb. The grandchild on the way. Despite everything we've given our children and tried to instill in them, Angie's made the same mistake."

"*Mistake?* We aren't a mistake, Will! Our children—none of them—are mistakes. And I don't think Angie would take kindly to you saying her baby is a mistake."

Will's sigh rumbled through the receiver against my ear. I pictured the exasperated expression that must be on his face. But although this wasn't the easiest of conversations, I was grateful as I always was when Will opened up.

I needed to bite my tongue and listen so he wouldn't think I was judging him or his opinions.

"I'm sorry, Deb. We should've had this conversation years ago and not in the middle of a blizzard. I can't even get home to talk to you in person."

"That's just as well." I didn't add that I thought maybe we were both cowards when it comes to spilling our guts.

"What are you thinking?" His tone was softer.

"Nothing. No, let me change that." I took a deep, steadying breath. "I'm thinking that you're stuck in your office with no reasonable amount of work to do, so you've redirected your type-A efforts toward me. It's giving you enough of a distraction to get through this time."

"That's not very nice, babe. You must think I'm a real bastard."

"C'mon, Will, you know that's not true."

Silence fell over the line and I stared out our bedroom window. I could barely see the outline of the fir trees in the distant yard. Too much snow obscured my view.

The ache in my chest had lightened, but I knew Will and I still had some talking to do.

"It's better that you're not here, or trying to get here. The wind's blowing like crazy."

I heard footsteps over the phone, and the clap of what must have been Will's window shades.

"Yeah, you're right. It's blowing all to hell here, too."

We each hung on, no words exchanged, but knowing he was on the line comforted me, even if he was still angry.

"We've been through a lot, haven't we, Will?"

"Yes."

"This is just another blip on the radar, isn't it?"

"Of course it is, honey. Why would you even think otherwise?"

"We can never take anything for granted. Didn't we learn that earlier than most?" I reminded him.

"Yes, yes, we did."

"I love you, Will."

"I love you, too."

And I knew he did. He'd always loved me, as I loved him.

But was it still enough, enough to sustain not just our partnership but also to buoy our children and now *their* kids, too?

"I need to go check on your mom."

"Aw, talk to me a bit more."

"What about?"

"Hell, I don't know. When's the exhibit?"

"In three weeks."

"Are you working on anything new or do you have all the pieces done?"

"Both. I'm going to include pieces from the chest, things I've made for spring and summer over the years, and I'm also working on a huge tapestry of the skyline."

By "skyline" I referred to the Buffalo night silhouette.

"How many days will it be at Albright-Knox?"

"A month. But I have to take it to New Orleans, Denver, Seattle and Atlanta after that."

"How far is the tapestry from being done?"

"One, maybe two weeks. I need to stay focused on getting it finished, but it's hard with all the other things I'm doing for the display."

"Don't forget you have more boxes of knitting in the attic."

Will's hint to clean up my storage made me laugh for the first time since we'd started this conversation.

"Yes, dear," I said demurely.

"Fine, laugh at me. But if you find a great idea for

your exhibit and it's too late to include it because you waited, don't blame me."

"Okay, I won't." Will loved to "help" me with my work.

"Talk to you later," he said.

"Bye."

CHAPTER TWENTY

Present Day
Buffalo, New York
Debra

I STAYED IN OUR ROOM for a while after I hung up with Will.

If I dwelled on our conversation I'd end up in a slump, or worse, too frazzled to get any work done.

I'd learned more patience with each year of being married to him, learned to be grateful for the times he opened up. When we were first married, he wasn't ready to talk about his emotions. And I wasn't ready to listen. All I wanted to do was fix things.

The garish half set of golf club covers stared up at me from the chest. I'd hung on to them as a means of punishing myself, I supposed.

Maroon and white, they were the colors of the high school the kids went to. And a reminder of the near-fatal blow the golf coach had been to my marriage.

Lyle Blackburn had been everything Will wasn't. Single, a long-term bachelor, earning the modest income of a public schoolteacher, supplemented by his tour on the pro circuit.

And white.

Shame pushed heat up my neck and face.

April 1989
Buffalo, New York

"GREAT DRIVE, BRIAN."

Lyle Blackburn clasped Brian's shoulder and smiled. "You'll take us to the state championships with that swing."

Debra watched the scene and wished Will could see how much Brian's stroke had improved. Will had been preoccupied with work, and she'd been so preoccupied with the kids' schedules and her own that she hadn't really filled him in.

"Hi, Debbie."

"Hey." She never corrected the nickname he used. It sounded so fresh, so alive, when he said it.

"Your boy's got real talent."

"Thanks." She smiled at Lyle and immediately berated herself. She was not going to be like all the other moms who ogled him. For heaven's sake, she'd been married for almost two decades! A new car or weaving loom was more appropriate for her than a lustful fantasy about Lyle Blackburn.

"Keep it up, Brian. Ten more and you're done for today."

"Okay, coach."

Lyle walked over to Debra and lightly grasped her arm. He guided her to a picnic bench not far from the driving range but far enough to give them some privacy.

"Have you ever golfed, Debbie?"

"No, I'm not really the athletic type."

"Golf isn't about athletics, Debbie. It's about the mental aspect. I even like to think it has a spiritual side."

Lyle's green eyes sparkled with the concentration Will once had. A complete focus, on her.

But she wasn't looking for a substitute.

"Coach Blackburn, I can barely keep up with my kids' schedules as it is. Fitting in four or five hours a week to hit a little white ball around the green isn't something I can do." Debra ignored his effusive charm.

"All the more reason to take some time for yourself."

Lyle looked at her, and Debra squirmed under his unabashed assessment.

"You do so much for Will and the kids. When's the last time someone did something for you?"

"I don't do more than any other wife." She pretended not to notice the sexual innuendo in his tone.

"Sure you do." He motioned at the area surrounding them. "How many wives and mothers do as much as you, Debbie? No one. The rest of the kids walk home every night. Not your boys."

Debra knew that. She often gave rides to Brian and Blair's classmates. But most of the other moms had real jobs, not artistic ones like hers.

"My work gives me a little more flexibility…"

"Stop making excuses for yourself. You're a great mom and you deserve a husband who worships you."

His come-on was kitschy, his method transparent. But Debra hadn't been the object of any adult atten-

tion—male attention—in so long that even Lyle's tacki-
ness boosted her ego.

Just a bit.

She got up from the table and said goodbye.

"I'm in the car when you're ready, Brian," she called.

She went to the station wagon and locked herself
inside. She needed something to remind her why she
stayed married to a man who worshipped his career
more than his wife.

Present Day
Buffalo, New York
Debra

"HELLO?" CALLER ID indicated it was Maggie from the
knitting group.

"Deb? I wanted to call and thank you for helping me
with Dave's sweater. I've managed to fix the entire
length of that dropped stitch."

"Good, I'm glad." I knew the sickening stomach
twist that occurred when a garment I'd been knitting for
weeks seemed to be ruined due to one mistake.

"Me, too! I was driving Dave crazy with my ranting
about how much work I'd done, and how I didn't think
I had it in me to start over."

"And you didn't have to, did you?" I smiled into the
phone. "You know, Maggie, it's so common to drop a
stitch. We all do it. You can get knitting so fast you don't
notice you've missed a stitch. I used to tell people to rip
out the whole thing, but why? We can fix it without all
the tears."

"Which takes time and patience, both of which you've spent on me. I can't thank you enough. How are you doing with the storm?"

"Great. Thanks for asking. I have my daughter and Will's mother over, so it's girl time. Plus, I have plenty to do with my work."

"Oh, I can't wait to see your exhibit, Deb!"

"And I can't wait for it to be done!"

We chatted a bit longer about our lives before we hung up.

It was gratifying to get a call from a young woman like Maggie. She may not realize it now, but our conversation was about knitting only on the surface.

Dropped stitches, like mistakes in life, abound.

And in marriage, there were opportunities for a great many dropped stitches.

Especially a marriage that's lasted as long as mine and Will's.

Will accused me of needing to "fix everything." But some days I just didn't have the patience or stamina to do the fixing part. I wanted to forget about it, shove the mistakes to the bottom of my knitting bag, so to speak.

But then the lure of the fiber, which in my marriage had always been our love and friendship, called me back.

And I found myself picking up the dropped stitch and weaving it back into the pattern of our life.

CHAPTER TWENTY-ONE

Present Day
Buffalo, New York

WILL STRETCHED OUT on the sofa bed in his office. He raised his wrist and looked at the gold watch Deb had given him for Christmas.

It was 5:30 a.m.

He yawned and swung his feet over the side of the bed. As far as hideaway beds went, this was the best. But it still wasn't the king-size, extra-firm mattress he shared with Deb.

Deb. He missed her. He relished waking up to her each morning, getting in that last kiss and cuddle before he had to start the day.

He missed her scent. Jasmine and her own feminine note.

The aroma of coffee entered his awareness. Obviously one of his colleagues had beaten him to it. Probably Vanessa.

All six curvy feet of her.

He scratched his head and stood up, stretching. That girl was one talented architect but clueless as to the personal side of life.

She was a Howard alumna, and never missed a chance to remind him of the one thing they had in common.

She was twenty-five years his junior, and he saw her more as a daughter. He wasn't stupid or ignorant of the fact that many colleagues his own age would take advantage of the situation.

But they didn't have a Deb at home. Chuck's wife of thirty-two years had died of breast cancer three years ago, and he was back in the market. Don had never professed to be a loyal husband and was known as a player. But Will didn't care what his employees and partners did with their personal lives, as long as it didn't affect the business.

That had been his stand since he started the firm almost thirty years ago.

Now he was going to be a grandfather. As he matured, he found it harder to keep his thoughts to himself. He wasn't judging his colleagues, not at all. But he wanted everyone to have a shot at the happiness he and Deb shared.

The truth was, it didn't come easy. And it was more than luck.

He'd always felt they had someone greater than them watching out for them. He and Deb had been greatly blessed along the way.

They'd also broken their backs trying to keep their marriage afloat.

Even soul mates had to work at it.

He tucked in his shirt and picked up the phone.

Deb's voice was sleepy but he didn't think he'd awakened her.

"Hi, babe."

"Good morning."

"How late were you gals up last night?"

"Your mother was asleep by ten. But Angie and I stayed up, talking."

"Solving all her problems?"

"Geez, what a great way to start the day, honey. Give me some credit. I'm not telling anyone what to do anymore."

Will stifled the chuckle that boiled up in his throat. The day Deb stopped caring about their children's happiness was a day he hoped would never come.

"You don't believe me, do you, Will?"

"Sure I do."

"Yeah, right. How does it look over there?"

Will raised his shades and stared out the huge pane of glass that comprised one wall of his office.

"Snow's still falling." The flakes weren't coming down as furiously as last night; he could see the streetlights' dim glow. But the snow fell nonetheless.

"Same here. It's supposed to stop by noon."

"Yeah. I should be home by seven or eight, as long as the temperatures hold and they get this cleaned up."

"I miss you, Will."

"I know."

"Who's at the office with you?"

"Chuck and Vanessa. Everyone else is in Arizona for that conference." The one he'd passed on. More and more he didn't want to travel if he didn't have to. Being home with Deb meant more to him.

"Hmm. I'll bet *she'd* love to have breakfast with you."

Will grunted. When it came to women he worked with, he'd learned the less said, the better.

"Sorry. You know I trust you, don't you?"

"Yes, of course." And she had no reason not to.

"It's just that I was a young woman once, and I understand the attraction an older man holds. The experience, the worldly knowledge."

"Maybe we'll get her to take a second look at Chuck."

"She needs someone her own age. Someone she can grow old with."

Deb didn't have to say "like us." Will knew what she meant.

"Well, I'd better have some coffee and get going on my work. If I can get out of here earlier, I will."

"Be safe, honey. I'll call you later."

"Bye."

"Bye."

Will smiled at the phone. God, he wished he was home. Funny how things worked out. As a young man getting his business off the ground, he'd certainly found home a comfort, but he'd also looked forward to the office every day. Especially when the kids were young.

He had to hand it to Deb—he couldn't have stayed home in what often seemed to be total chaos. Yet Deb had done it and done it well. She thrived on the constant change and activity, even managed to keep her art going, albeit on a part-time basis for a while there.

Now, as an older guy, he liked home best. He had an office there and worked in it whenever he could, when he didn't have to come in to the downtown location.

But Deb wanted to get out more, probably because

she'd been home all those years. It was as though their roles had been reversed.

He understood, but at times it perplexed him that she didn't want to stay in more, with him.

Maybe he needed to give her a reason....

A knock at his door interrupted his thoughts.

"Come in."

"Good morning, Will."

Vanessa entered. Her blouse had been pressed and her skirt showed nary a wrinkle. She even had her high-heeled shoes back on.

"Good morning, Vanessa."

"I figured you'd like some coffee." She handed him a steaming mug and set a plate with a bagel and cream cheese on the service table near his chair.

"Thanks, but you didn't have to do this." Usually Lori, his personal assistant, took care of the coffee, but she hadn't made it into work since the day before yesterday. She lived south of the city, and they usually got the brunt of the lake-effect storms.

"I wanted to."

She smiled at him and Will wondered, not for the first time, if she realized she acted like a doe in heat around him. Or maybe she did this around all the men in the office—he hadn't bothered to take note.

"I'm going to wrap up the plans for the mall in Schenectady. I'll have them on your desk by close of business today."

"Fine. But keep an eye on the weather. If we can leave earlier, we will. We all need a break, and I don't want to risk being stuck here again tonight."

Disappointment flickered in her brown eyes, but Will gave her credit for masking it with a weak smile.

"Sure thing."

She turned and left and started to shut his door.

"Leave it open, Vanessa."

"No problem."

Will went to his desk and fired up his computer. Thank God they hadn't lost power this time out. As far as Buffalo storms went, this was proving to be a manageable one.

ANGIE WATCHED VI DOZE on the sofa, wrapped in the tattered shawl Mom had made her years ago. Her face was soft, even with the lines of her life etched across it.

Angie finished her coffee and looked around. Mom had already disappeared into her studio.

Angie found her there, on her stool in front of the weaving frame, her tapestry almost finished.

"It's beautiful, Mom." Angie studied the colors of the sunrise over the Buffalo skyline; it served as the backdrop to a huge maple tree, divided into the four seasons—bare branches, buds and "helicopter" seeds, green glossy leaves, flamboyant autumnal hues.

Angie laughed, and Debra looked up and offered her a smile.

"Good morning, sweetheart. What's so funny?"

"The twins and I used to play for hours with the maple seeds—we called them 'helicopters.' Do you remember, Mom?"

Debra chuckled as she kept weaving. "What I remember is finding the boys with firecrackers right after they blew up their G.I. Joe fort in the sandbox."

Angie giggled. "I was hiding in the shed—who do you think gave them the matches?"

Debra smiled again, kept working.

"How much more do you have to do?"

"Just these last few inches. It'll be ready well ahead of the exhibit."

Angie watched her mother's hands moving quickly and confidently, and thought of all the wonderful things those hands had created over the years.

Like Grandma Violet's shawl....

"Mom, how bad was it when you told Grandma Vi you and Daddy were getting married?"

Debra raised her head and rested the shuttle on the frame.

"Bad. As we've told you kids, it all happened when your granddad passed away. His heart was getting weaker, and the stress of it all sent him over the edge."

"You don't really believe it's your fault or Daddy's that he died, do you?"

Debra met Angie's eyes.

"No, it wasn't anyone's 'fault,' Angie, but maybe we could've handled it differently."

"Like how?"

Debra swiped at her forehead in an effort to get the curls out of her face. Angie saw the tired lines in her face, the circles under her eyes. Mom had always thrived on her art, but like any work, it took its toll.

"Maybe we should've just eloped. Not told anyone. Gone off to California." She gave Angie a gentle smile.

"You mean like I did?" Angie had felt awful when she'd first told Debra and Will that she and Jesse had been married in San Francisco City Hall. But then they'd had a church blessing and huge family reception in Buffalo, which had overjoyed her parents.

Angie nodded; their decision had really had more to do with Jesse and *his* parents, which Debra understood.

"But you somehow brought Grandma around—how did you do it?"

"I didn't do it, Angie, Violet did. She brought herself around. And I imagine you had something to do with it."

"Me?"

"Yes, you. You spent a lot of time with her, especially when the twins were born. Vi would either come and get you or I'd drop you off and you'd have a girls' day. I think it was good for her, since Will's brother and sister had already moved out and across the country."

"Uncle Jimmy came back for visits—he still does." Angie loved her retired army uncle. He told the best stories, and his wife, Doris, was a doll. They'd never had any kids themselves, so they'd treated Angie and the boys like their own whenever they were in town, which admittedly wasn't all that often.

"Yes, he did, but it's not the same. You see that now, don't you? Look how much time we've spent together in the two months since you've been back—more than the past ten years combined!"

"It must have been hard for Grandma Vi. Especially since her only daughter moved halfway around the world." Will's sister had joined the foreign service and when she was in the U.S. on a rare tour, it was never in Buffalo.

"Yes, but I'll give Vi credit. She's always loved you unconditionally. That first year or two, she didn't say much to me, but she always had a smile, a hug and a kiss for you."

"What about your mom?"

"She just doesn't have it to give, honey. She cares about you and the boys, but since my father left, she's never been the same, even after marrying Fred. They're content as they are, and that's fine with me. I've had my hands full with your dad and his family."

"I wish you'd had siblings like me, Mom. Blair and Brian have helped me through so much."

"I'm not alone, Angie. I've had friends like the knitting gals, my work colleagues and of course your dad. Now that you're an adult, I have you. What more could I ask for?"

Angie knew Debra's belief was genuine, but her heart still ached for her mother.

"Wouldn't you do anything to keep what you have with Jesse?" Debra's query jolted Angie out of her put-Mom-on-a-pedestal thoughts.

"Mom, it's completely different!"

"Is it? Jesse's folks weren't too happy with you at first. They've mellowed because you were kind and gracious to them."

"Yes, but—"

"And now you're going to have Jesse's baby. Isn't that worth keeping a family together for?"

Angie groaned. "Mom, I told you I didn't want to talk about this. I'm dealing with it."

"You're the one who came in here needing answers. I'm out of the advice business, but here's a suggestion from your mom—don't drag things out longer than you need to, and don't make them a bigger deal than they have to be. Just do the next right thing."

"And that would be?" Angie immediately wished she hadn't asked. She didn't want a full-blown lecture from Debra, nor did she want her to think she was requesting guidance.

But Debra didn't do anything she normally would have.

She smiled. "That's for you to figure out." Debra picked up the shuttle and resumed weaving.

"Where did you get the idea for the tree?"

"It's based on the Belgian tapestries that depict the tree of life. In a sense, it's our family tree."

"How?"

"Well, our family has several living generations, and you can look at generations like seasons. But I prefer to see each of us as a separate branch, sprouting our own leaves, holding our own nests, waving in the winds of life. I think we go through the seasons several different times during our lives, while the tree, the family tree, stays constant and steady through it all. It's about the love that connects us, Angie. Not just blood ties or names."

June 1974
Buffalo, New York

DEBRA GLANCED at her reflection one last time. Her hair was in place, the tendrils she'd coaxed into corkscrews hung on either side of her face. Her makeup was the "natural" look with peach blusher and lip gloss.

Funny how having a baby had made her feel more like a woman than ever. Of course, Will's presence back in her life didn't hurt, either. When he'd found her in Boston, Angie had only been three weeks old; she was just over six weeks today. Debra's doctor had given her the green light for sex.

But she didn't know if she could deal with Will seeing her. She was still heavy, and her breasts felt like watermelons under the peasant-style wedding dress. All Debra could think of was the myriad stretch marks on the sides of her breasts and across her lower belly. She had no doubt that Will loved her but he hadn't been there during her pregnancy and the birth. He couldn't possibly appreciate what her body had been through.

Would he accept her as she was?

"What, sweetpea? Mommy's here." She'd just fed Angie, but the little peanut was hungry again. Debra looked at the clock on her nightstand.

Ten-thirty.

The church was five minutes away, and she wasn't due there until a quarter to. She decided to feed Angie now so she'd sleep through the ceremony.

As she cushioned Angie at her breast she swallowed a twinge of guilt. If she'd let Will in on her pregnancy and they'd married sooner, this might be Angie's baptism. As it was, they were going to baptize her in a couple of weeks. Debra wanted to be married when Angie was baptized, and Will agreed.

She'd done the right thing, she hoped. This way she knew Will had come back for *her* and wanted to marry her even before he'd learned about Angie.

Debra eased Angie over to her other breast. Ten thirty-seven. She'd make it, no problem.

She looked around the tiny motel room while Angie suckled. Thank God she and Will were moving into their apartment immediately after the wedding. It wasn't much, but it was clean and in a safe part of Buffalo, near the university.

They both agreed it would be the most open-minded place to settle and start their life together. And it wasn't too far from Will's office. It also had a small extra room Debra planned to use as a studio.

She'd studied art history but her passion over the past year had turned toward fiber arts. She wasn't fond of the current macramé pop art and wanted to help preserve more traditional fiber arts like weaving and knitting.

It seemed odd to be in this nondescript motel room instead of the house she'd grown up in. But her mother refused to have anything to do with the wedding. She hadn't even held Angie yet. It cut through Debra's heart when her mother said, "I can't believe I have a mulatto grandchild. I raised you better."

Debra had left the house of her childhood with Angie in her arms, tears of pride in her eyes.

But she wasn't without resources. She'd saved some money from her teaching assistant job the past year, and paid to stay in this room for a week.

Angie's cry for attention brought her back to the present.

"It's okay. Let's go." She lifted her daughter and nestled her against one shoulder. While she patted Angie's back and waited for the needed burp, Debra realized that this was what it all meant. This was what mattered.

Having a healthy baby. A baby with two parents who loved her and had the means to support her. It might not be in the style Will was used to, but it wouldn't be the unhealthy emotional environment Debra had known, either.

WILL WAITED IN THE FOYER of the church. It was time for Debra and Angie to be here. He should've put his foot down and insisted on picking her up, the hell with tradition.

He purposely hadn't called his mother this morning. Or yesterday. He'd wanted to give her another chance, to see if the mother he knew she *could* be would emerge from the anger and grief. To see if this horrible break in their relationship could be mended.

No such luck.

He wanted today to be special. For him and Deb, and of course, Angie.

His sister was still living at home with Mama, and his brother was away at army summer training, so he wouldn't have any guests. Neither would Deb.

Fine. They'd start this journey on their own. With their love, faith and the friendship that had sustained them all these years since they were little kids.

Sure, the great friendship that had her keep your own child from you.

His gut tensed.

He had to let it go. It was his fault as much as Debra's that they hadn't been together when Angie was born.

He saw her blue Chevy Nova pull into the church parking lot. His bride, his child. He wished he could turn back time. He wished he'd gone to Boston sooner. She hadn't answered any of his letters; they'd all been returned, stamped Address Unknown. And he hadn't been able to find her address through directory assistance. He'd only had her phone number. He told himself again that he should've driven up there sooner.

But the day's drive was more than he could have handled. Between closing Dad's office, dealing with the finances, being vetted for partner at the city's leading architectural firm and looking in on Mama, it'd been too much.

No, he couldn't focus on that. He and Debra were together again, and Angie was their beautiful daughter. Mama might never get over his marriage to Debra, but he'd bet his future partnership that she wouldn't be able to resist Angie. Not for long.

CHAPTER TWENTY-TWO

Present Day
Buffalo, New York

TO WILL'S RELIEF, the storm had passed and he was on his way home. He talked to the voice-activated cellphone system in his car. "Call Angie."

"Dialing Angie," the smooth digital voice of the hands-free system replied.

"Hello?"

"Hi, babe. You still at the house?"

"Yeah, they didn't get the plows out here yet."

"Sorry, Angie. I know you're trying to get yourself established at the station."

"Yeah, well, that's how it goes."

Was that acceptance in his daughter's voice?

"Can you stay put at least until I get there?"

"Uh, sure, Dad. What's up?"

"I want to talk to you about something."

"Fine. See you in a bit."

"Tell your mother I'm on my way."

He disconnected and kept his eyes on the still-treacherous roads. It wasn't like him to tell his kids what to do, but this was different.

He couldn't handle Angie and Jesse making the same mistake he and Deb had.

ANGIE WENT DOWNSTAIRS to the family room. Grandma Vi had gone back to her cottage. She said she needed a decent rest after sleeping in the guest room, which made Angie laugh. Grandma Vi was her own person as much as she'd ever been.

Her mother was in her studio, so she didn't hear the door open when Will came in.

Angie went over and gave him a hug.

"Hi, Daddy."

"Hey, baby."

He shrugged out of his coat. "I'll bet you're wondering why I need to talk to you so badly."

"Not really. I imagine it has something to do with me and Jesse?"

"You got it. Where's your mother?"

Dad could never be away from Mom for very long.

"In her studio."

"Let me go say hello and then we'll sit down. Do you mind making us some tea?"

"Not at all, Daddy."

Angie measured out the jasmine tea that was her father's favorite. Will came back into the room just as she was pouring the boiling water over the infusers.

He sat at the kitchen counter. Angie walked around and sat next to him.

"What's up, Dad?"

"Angie, your life is yours. You know how I feel about that. And I like Jesse—he's a good man." Will paused and took a sip of the hot tea. "But I also know that you two will work it out. This is what marriage is all about."

"Dad, please." First Mom, now Dad. She'd had enough of this. She was thirty-five, not fifteen.

"Hear me out, baby girl. Your mother and I were in somewhat similar circumstances, oh—" he looked up at the wall and stroked his chin "—about thirty-six years ago."

"I know, Mom told me. She's never really hidden it from us—the boys and I noticed years ago that your anniversary date and my birthday are awfully close. I just never put it together until Mom told me the whole story at the café."

"Yes, they are." Will smiled at Angie, and she felt the intensity of his love in every word. "I've never held this against your mother, Angie, or I've tried not to, but the fact that I didn't get to share the pregnancy with her, or be there for your birth, well…" He shook his head. "I wish I'd been given a choice. That's all."

"You would've married Mom right away?"

"Of course. And I would've been there for her. *With* her. What if she'd died? Or you hadn't made it? How would I have felt then, after the fact?"

Angie stared at her father. He'd never talked to her about this before and she felt uneasy. It seemed too personal, too private.

"Dad, all's well that ends well. You and Mom got married. You raised us. I never knew any differently until I was an adult, and then I could handle it. The most important thing is that you two stayed together."

"Honey, I'm not complaining. I'm just saying it

would've been nice if I'd been given an option to be a participant in your life from the get-go. For me, for you and for your mom."

"But Mom knows you love her. You always have."

"Of course she does. But love isn't just about knowing, Angie. It's about doing."

Her father drank more of his tea and drummed his fingers on the table. "If you love or have ever loved Jesse, if you love the baby growing inside you, you have to give it all a chance. And that starts with telling Jesse. *Now.*"

Angie blinked. "I'm supposed to meet him in Paris. I'll tell him there."

"You handle it how you want, sweetheart, but handle it. Don't put it off. If you're not going to Paris in the next few days, you have to tell him now."

Angie didn't agree with her father. She thought it was best to tell Jesse in person. But this wasn't the time to argue about it.

She placed her hand on his shoulder. "Thanks, Dad. I know this wasn't easy for you."

He nodded and stared down at his mug. "I just want you to give it *all* a chance, Angie."

Present Day
Buffalo, New York
Debra

THE NEXT MORNING came too quickly. Will insisted on going to work, even though he'd barely made it home the night before.

After Will left, I spent most of the morning working in the studio.

Until Angie called me from her cell. But she was here in the house, wasn't she?

"Mom! Grandma's having a hard time breathing."

Angie had obviously gone back to the cottage to see Vi.

I threw down the phone and ran out the back kitchen door toward the cottage.

I took the shortest route across the lawn.

It wasn't shoveled like the pathway. I had to lift my knees high to get through the deep snow.

My slippers weren't meant for snowshoeing but there wasn't time to change into boots.

Rose barked wildly, running ahead to get to the cottage. Her barks spiked my alarm as she always seemed to sense when Vi wasn't doing well.

Once I reached the cottage and opened the door, I saw that Vi was hunched over on the couch, gasping for air. Angie was massaging her back, cooing to her.

"It's okay, Grandma. Help's coming. Mom's here."

"Hey, Vi. What's going on?"

I knelt beside her but she only spared me a glance. She needed all her energy to get oxygen.

"Tight...chest...hurts."

"Hang on."

I went into her kitchen and got her emergency meds, then grabbed the oxygen tank from the pantry.

"Let's get you hooked up."

Angie continued to stroke Vi's back while I got her on the oxygen and gave her the drugs I'd been instructed to.

"You'll feel better soon."

Even as I said it, Vi's complexion pinked up.

She always refused any outside help except for me and Will. A permanent care facility could've been an option but not for Will's mother. Or for us. Not as long as we could take care of her.

When her breathing evened out and she was more relaxed, leaning back on the couch, I spoke.

"Vi, this is why it's important to use the oxygen and take your meds each day. It'll prevent these crises."

She waved her hand in front of her face.

"It doesn't matter. I'm going to die sooner than later."

"Grandma!" Angie hated Vi's talk of death. But Vi had claimed she'd be joining her dear departed husband "soon" for the past thirty-six years, since his death.

"Vi, we're all going to die. But there's no need to go out before we have to or with this kind of suffering."

Her gaze locked on mine. I saw her pain, her frustration. She'd always been the maestro, orchestrating her own life—or at least thought she was. Now even the illusion of control was gone.

"Just let me lie here. If the good Lord wants me, He can take me now."

Gently I lifted her feet and swung her around so she could lie full-length on the couch. I reached over her and tugged down the afghan I'd knitted her, placing it around her. The shades of browns and purples accented her pallor but also brought out the amber flecks in her brown eyes.

"The good Lord isn't taking you anywhere right now," I said briskly as I tucked the edge of the blanket under the sofa cushions.

"You don't know that."

"No, I don't. But you're looking a heck of a lot better than you did fifteen minutes ago."

Vi sniffed and rolled onto her side. "Where's the remote? It's time for my show."

Yes, she was definitely feeling better.

"Here, Grandma."

"I'll make you some tea," I said.

I went into her kitchen and made enough tea for all three of us. Vi needed to come over to our house and stay there. But she'd fight me on it. I decided to wait and have Will tell her instead.

Vi's days were numbered, and I tried to remind myself that it was no different for any of us. But I couldn't lie. Her doctor had told us a year ago that this time would come, when the congestive heart failure she'd suffered for so long would attack with a vengeance.

And her eighty-five-year-old body wouldn't be able to fend it off.

As we sat there and sipped tea and tried to help Vi get some down, I mused that my own mother was the same age but appeared twenty years younger. Yet my mother never spent much time with us. Her interest in her grandchildren was fleeting at best.

And here Vi, who'd fought tooth and nail to keep Will and me apart, had become an integral part of our family.

Once I felt she'd come through the worst of her episode, I left Angie with Vi and went back to the house to call Will.

"Your mother had a spell, honey."

"How bad was it?"

"She's okay now, but it was scary for all of us. Thank God Angie was over there."

I heard his sigh, felt the heaviness in his heart.

"We're lucky we've had her this long," he said.

"Yes, we are. But it doesn't make this any easier."

"Do you think we should take her to the doctor?"

"I'm going to call him now. He said he'd be willing to come out here if we ever need him, but honestly, I'm pretty sure we're okay. He's not going to tell us anything different, and I followed all his instructions."

"Yeah, well, thanks for doing this, honey. Do you want me to come home now?"

What he was really asking me was, "Will my mother still be alive when I get there?"

"No, I think she's fine now. You may want to call her in a bit." I took a deep breath and let it out slowly.

"What aren't you telling me, babe?"

"Will, she needs to come live with us. Even the cottage is too far away. If Angie hadn't been there, she could have died."

The act of uttering those words made my heart beat faster. In some ways, I thought I was detached from Vi, despite our years of mending fences. But she was Will's mother. And she'd been more of a mother to me than my own.

"Can you and Angie get her to the house now?"

"Honey, you know your mama. She's not going to come over here unless you're the one calling the shots. It's not a problem. Angie and I will sit with her through the day, and you can bring her over tonight."

"All right." His business tone was back in place. The

news had scared him, but we'd both known for a while that this time was coming.

"See you later, honey."

"Bye."

What I didn't want to talk about over the phone was the obvious. Anytime in the past when Vi had a spell like this, she'd called the house or my cell phone immediately.

She hadn't this time. If Angie hadn't walked over to watch the soap with Vi, it could have been a different day altogether.

My fingers itched to knit. I needed the rhythm of the needles and yarn between my fingers to soothe my racing mind. If I wasn't calm, I wouldn't be able to keep Violet comfortable and at ease.

And Angie had to be kept calm, too.

I changed my wet socks and sweatpants and put on my favorite comfort socks with jeans. I'd knitted the socks several years back, and the cashmere yarn was soft against my feet. It was not politically correct to buy cashmere these days, because of the dust clouds caused by those huge herds of goats in China. So I was glad I made the socks guilt-free when I did.

With Will's sweater and more yarn stuffed into my tote bag, along with some tuna sandwiches I'd quickly made, I headed back to Vi's.

The snow sparkled under the sun. As bright as the sun looked, it didn't warm up the temperature, which had stayed well below freezing for over a week. We were having a rough end of winter.

At least the storm had passed, and I heard the plows

in the distance. They'd have our street cleared soon, but until then Vi, Angie and I could enjoy the afternoon together. I swallowed some tears, along with the thought that this could be our last time....

WILL LOOKED OUT at the street in front of his office. He'd made it in this morning only because he had four-wheel drive, but had called the house and told Angie to stay put—the highway to where she worked was still blocked and he saw no reason for his daughter and future grandchild to be at risk.

He should've stayed home today. He could have. But he'd left out of habit. He was also feeling a little closed in, with the intensity of Deb, his mother and Angie all together.

Just a few weeks ago he'd cursed his younger sister for not being here for Mama. She lived in Africa with her husband—her four kids were grown and gone. Jimmy and his wife were in South Carolina, where he'd retired from the U.S. Army. It was too far to expect them to come up here regularly and they couldn't drop everything each time Mama had a spell.

She'd never leave Buffalo. Her roots were here, and her ties to Dad's memories.

It hadn't been easy, caring for Vi, dealing with her quirks and her hatred of his marriage to Debra in the early years.

But he was glad that Mama had Deb. That they were together—and that he'd been able to do what his father had asked.

Take care of Mama.

Deb had played a huge part in this, and he didn't give her enough credit. Plenty of other women would've walked out on him, just to get away from his family. Not Debra.

Again, she was his rock.

The very fact that Mama allowed Debra to tend her spoke of a trust that no one would have ever believed.

Violet Bradley had given Debra a hard time, that was for sure. But Vi didn't count on the quality in Debra that had attracted Will since they were kids.

Her genuine care for other people. Whether it was a kid on the bus or Will or a stranger in the grocery store, Debra *cared* about how they were in that moment she shared with them. Will loved Debra for her compassion but hated when it turned to taking care of others at her own expense. He'd seen her run herself ragged over the years and end up with no time for him and the kids. And no time for Debra. Will loved it when she felt fulfilled, taking care of herself. She glowed with life and love and was a bigger, better version of the woman he'd married.

Will chuckled to himself.

He wasn't the only one who couldn't resist Debra's big green eyes, wide-open and sparkling with compassion.

Mama had just taken a while, that was all.

CHAPTER TWENTY-THREE

August 1979
Buffalo, New York

SEVEN MONTHS PREGNANT, Debra waddled down the driveway of their Cape Cod colonial and shoved herself behind the steering wheel of the aqua Chevy Nova.

Angie was wrapping up her morning at Grandma Vi's. Of course, Violet never spoke to Debra, never made eye contact. After repeated failed attempts at hosting a family dinner, Debra told Will to take Angie to his mother's.

Debra couldn't tolerate the hostility anymore.

But she knew that Violet had fallen in love with Angie the first time she'd seen her, right after the wedding. Violet's eyes had still been burning with rage at Debra and only softened marginally when she glanced at Will. But the sight of her first grandchild with mocha skin and sweet baby curls had melted a good portion of the glacier that was her heart.

Not that Debra received any of the warmth.

Debra drove the few miles to Violet's house, where Will had grown up. She and Will had chosen to live closer to the suburbs and hoped to be out near Orchard Park or East Aurora before too long. They needed one more good year with his business.

It'd been rough with the recession, but Will's talent and hard work had paid off in hard-won contracts for several shopping malls around the country.

The heat of the day was in full swing as she pulled up in front of Violet's huge entryway. Debra sighed. The babies jostled for position and one little foot connected with her rib cage.

"Ooof." She rubbed her belly.

Once she'd managed to hoist herself out of the car, she walked around to the passenger side and opened the door. She reached in for the package on the seat. Wrapped in white paper with tiny violets printed all over it was the shawl she'd knitted Vi. She'd actually knitted it years ago, when she and Will were just married and Angie was crawling around on the floor at her feet.

But only today did she have the nerve to give it to Vi.

Today was the anniversary of Will's father's death. And it was too hot for Violet to even entertain the idea of using the shawl. But Debra was sick of the constant tension. This was her attempt to negotiate a peace.

Before she could get to the front door, the screen swung open and Angie ran out. "Hi, Mommy!"

Angie hugged Debra's knees so tight, Debra had to hang on to the door of the car so they wouldn't buckle.

"Hi, sweetheart. Did you have a good time?"

"Yes, Grandma Vi and me ate san'witches and drank l'monade and watched *General 'opital*."

"You watched *General Hospital?*" Debra was grateful her five-year-old wouldn't have understood most of the soap opera's goings-on.

"Uh-huh." Angie's curls rasped against Debra's legs. Debra looked at the front door. Vi wasn't in sight. She didn't come out unless Will was with them, or unless she absolutely had to.

Debra squared her shoulders. Enough was enough.

"Let's go back in for a minute, honey."

"Okay, Mommy. But Grandma already said bye."

Clutching her daughter's hand, Debra walked up to the door and peered in. Vi wasn't in the foyer or the living room, either. She didn't want to barge in and startle Vi, so she rang the doorbell.

The huge gong made Angie giggle. "That sounds like our church bell, Mommy."

"Yes, it does, sweetie."

Vi's steps were unmistakable, the shuffle of her feet in house slippers rhythmic against the hardwood floors.

She rounded the corner and Debra acted as though she'd been studying Vi's front garden all along.

When Vi reached the door, she didn't say anything. She didn't open the door, either.

Part of Debra wished it was winter so she'd have glass between them instead of just the screen. Vi's negativity unnerved her.

"Hey, Vi. Thanks for having Angie over today."

"She's my granddaughter, aren't you, baby?" Vi cooed at Angie, completely ignoring Debra.

Debra leaned over as best she could with her bulge of a stomach and spoke in a quiet tone to Angie.

"The car's in the shade and the windows are open. Why don't you wait for me there, honey? I'll be over in a minute."

"Okay, Mommy." Angie smiled at Vi again. "Bye Grandma." She skipped to the open passenger door and climbed into the backseat, where several teddy bears were arrayed.

Once Debra was sure Angie was out of earshot, she turned to Violet again, who still stood at the screen door.

"I've got something for you, Vi."

"Any reason?" The condescension in Vi's tone sent chills of warning down Debra's back.

"Many reasons, actually. I thought you might like a little gift to cheer you up today."

"Nothing will ever cheer me up from the loss of my husband. If you and Will—"

"Violet, I've had enough of this. You're the grand-mother of my daughter and of these two boys inside me. You don't have to like me, but you're going to have to accept me. I'm not going anywhere. I love your son. Can you focus on that?"

Debra's anger gave her the momentum and courage to look directly at Violet, something she didn't think she'd ever done before.

"You have no idea what I've been through."

"No, I don't. But I can imagine. If anything happened to Will, I'd—" Tears welled up and her throat tightened.

"You're lucky all you have to do is imagine." Violet's tone was just as hard, but Debra detected a note of another kind. Was there even a glimmer of a chance that Violet would crack, maybe a fraction of an inch, and let her in?

"I suppose your mother's thrilled about the new babies." Violet nodded at Debra's belly.

"No, actually, she's never been happy with me since Will and I got married."

"I understand."

No, she didn't understand, but Debra wasn't about to go into her own family's issues. Debra's mother didn't like Will, not just because he was black but because she saw how happy Debra was with him. Linda had never got over her bitterness at her husband's leaving. She couldn't be happy for Debra because she had no happiness for herself.

"I'm tired of it, Vi. All the bickering, the blaming. I loved Will's father, too, you know. He gave my mother that job all those years ago and kept us off food stamps and welfare."

"He was always doing for the less fortunate."

Irritation made another swipe at Debra's composure but she ignored it. Violet couldn't keep herself from consigning Debra and her "kind" to their "place."

Debra sighed. "I know it's too hot for this now—" she held the package out to Violet "—but I hope you'll appreciate it when fall comes."

Violet stared at the offered gift as though it were hot coals ready to sear her hands. Debra watched the emotions on Violet's face. Stubbornness, pride, sorrow, exhaustion. No regret, but Debra knew better than to expect too great of a miracle.

All Debra prayed for was a tiny one—that Violet would take the damned shawl.

Violet clucked her tongue. Debra was about to turn

and go, but she saw Vi raise her skinny arm and unlatch the screen door.

She opened it just far enough to take the gift Debra had painstakingly wrapped. Vi didn't open the door any farther, nor did she even say "thanks."

But she took the gift. That was enough for Debra.

"We'll see you next week."

Debra walked back to the car. Vi didn't knit, so she wouldn't understand how much work had gone into the shawl or the intricate pattern Debra had designed for her.

But it didn't matter.

Violet had accepted the gift.

Present Day
Buffalo, New York
Debra

THE REST OF THE AFTERNOON went smoothly. I'd spoken with Vi's doctor, who assured me I'd handled things correctly. There was nothing to do at this point except to make Vi comfortable. She could live another day, a year or a decade. Such was the aging process and the effects of congestive heart disease.

"Okay, ladies, I'm going to get our dinner in the oven." I put down my knitting and stretched. "Anyone need anything?"

"I think I'll eat dinner here tonight," Violet said, but her eyes never left the screen. The shopping channel was displaying its "best of the best" housecoats.

"We'll see. Let me go figure out what it is!"

I gave Vi a peck on the cheek and squeezed Angie's arm. Angie smiled at me, a smile that said, "Don't worry, I'm here with her."

I walked back to the house with Rosie at my heels.

"You're hungry, too, aren't you, girl?"

The golden retriever wagged her tail and her whole body shook, even though she was shoulder-deep in snow.

Once inside, I set about making dinner. I pulled the salmon steaks out of the refrigerator and grabbed the fresh dill I'd bought at the gourmet store.

Then I tidied up the family room and as I folded Vi's old shawl, I smiled to myself.

Talk about a lifetime ago.

When I'd knitted that shawl for Vi, I'd been intent on proving to her how worthy I was to be Will's wife. That I was different, and that my being white wasn't going to hurt Will or our children, not if I could do anything about it.

Of course, it hadn't just been Violet's fault that I'd harbored this deep fear of failing Will or the kids. I'd done it to myself with my constant worry that my up-bringing couldn't be overcome. That even though I'd attended one of our nation's top colleges, I'd never get over growing up on the wrong side of Buffalo.

As Will and I faced the prejudice that a relationship like ours could bring, I became obsessed with protecting my children from it. Too much so. They needed to know the world wasn't perfect and that there would always be those who'd single them out for being from a racially blended family.

Thank God times had changed!

But I never stopped worrying about my children.

Blair and Brian had experienced the type of racism any African-American child in a mostly white suburban setting would, but they had risen above it, and as the other kids had gotten to know them they'd gained the respect and admiration of their classmates

Angie had had it tougher. Girls can be mean to each other, especially in junior and senior high. Unlike her twin brothers, Angie hadn't had athletics to ease the pain of her shyness or her adolescent insecurities. Her uncertain racial identification, because of her pale skin and dark, curly hair, had made her the victim of some cruel jokes. I'd felt so guilty in those years—still did, if I examined my heart.

But then…if I hadn't married him, our children wouldn't have been born at all. And Angie wouldn't have her grandmother's café-au-lait skin, and Blair wouldn't have Will's shoulders or Brian his adept hands.

I held the shawl to my face and breathed in. I'd sat for so many nights crying and knitting my tears into this yarn. I'd longed for Violet to know the love Will and I had rediscovered in Paris. We were determined to thrive here in Western New York.

All these years later, I no longer had to tell her. She knew.

So why hadn't I been able to let go of the past and my worries about the kids? They'd all grown up and were on their way to wonderful lives and families of their own.

Angie was going to work things out with Jesse, I was sure of it. She just had to get over her fears of rejection and her excessive need for independence. Blair and

Stella would have a baby soon enough, God willing, and Brian would find his life's partner in due time.

It would all work out. I had to believe that.

CHAPTER TWENTY-FOUR

Present Day
Buffalo, New York

WILL LOOKED AROUND the dinner table. His aging
mother sat next to him, her face relaxed and her smile
comfortable despite what she'd been through today.

His daughter, Angie, three months pregnant with
his first grandchild, sat on his other side, chatting with
his mother.

Debra, his wife and mate of more than thirty-five
years, sat opposite him. She'd been quiet tonight, just
answering a few questions here and there.

From this angle and with the aid of the candlelight
on the table, Debra looked almost identical to the way
she had when he'd met her again in Paris. Her red locks
were enhanced by a bottle now, but they were the same
sun-streaked curls that had caught his eye in the Paris
classroom. The same curls he'd grown used to gazing
down at whenever he walked her home from the bus
stop.

Her eyes were beautiful seas of green that he'd will-
ingly lost himself in thousands of times over the years.

Her mouth wasn't smiling tonight, though. Maybe the storm and taking care of Mama had been a little much for her. And she was worried about her exhibit, no doubt.

"Hey, hon, how's it going with your show?"

"Fine. Well, I still have some work to do, but it'll all come together."

Will smiled.

"That's what you always say when it's stressing you out."

Deb offered a weak smile.

"Yes, I suppose that's true." She put down the fork that had been pushing her casserole around. "Actually, I may change it."

"But, Mom, your show's only two weeks away!"

Angie understood what her mother put into each art event.

"I know. But all I have to really finish is my current weaving. I'm using other stuff from over the years as the basis of the display."

"Want to use my shawl?" Violet cackled at her own joke. The shawl was so tattered from Vi's constant use, especially in cold weather.

"Thanks for the offer, Vi." Debra smiled.

Will couldn't keep the grin off his face. His three women all at the same table, all smiling.

And Mama was still here with them.

Life didn't get any better.

ANGIE WENT BACK to the guest room after dinner and packed her bag. Dad had brought Grandma Vi over to the house and the roads were clear. She could go home.

The storm had given her time to rethink her situation with Jesse. It was one thing to let her pride keep *her* from having a relationship with him but to keep the baby from knowing his or her father—that was pure thievery.

She shoved her few clothes and toiletries into her large tote, but her fingers paused on the ivory prayer shawl Mom had made her when she'd gone to college.

She played with the soft wool and marveled at how detailed her mother's stitches were. Angie loved to knit, too, but would never master the art as her mother had. Few people did.

The shawl had comforted her through so much.

She remembered when she'd gone to college— excited, afraid. But it was just the beginning....

And then she'd met Jesse.

She shook her head and placed the shawl in her tote. Work was calling, and after that she'd have to start preparing for her trip to Paris.

Debra

"YOU MADE A GREAT DINNER, honey." I was already in bed.

"Thanks, Will. I'm glad you convinced Vi to stay over."

"I don't know how much I convinced her. She's a stubborn woman. It wouldn't surprise me if tomorrow she decides she's going to live in the cottage on her own again."

I sighed and put down the latest issue of my favorite fiber arts magazine. "She doesn't have a choice anymore, I'm afraid. You know that, don't you?"

Will's face was stoic, but I saw the sadness in his eyes. "Yeah, I do."

"Come here." I patted the comforter.

Will complied and laid his head on my chest. I rubbed his arms and ran my fingers through his hair. I felt the relaxation seep through him.

"I suppose we all think our parents will somehow live forever," he murmured.

"My mother will, mark my words."

"Aw, honey, even your mother's getting older. We all are."

"Vi's had a good life, Will. It was horrible for her to be widowed so young, but she made her choices. She could've remarried or at least dated."

"Never. Not after my father."

"Will, I understand that, but we all have needs."

Will turned his head and looked into my eyes.

"Are you telling me that if I croak you'll take up with someone?"

"I'm saying that if either of us goes, then the other should know it's okay to find someone else. It doesn't have to be the same kind of love—it can't be. But why should a widowed spouse be lonely the rest of his or her life?"

Will chuckled. "You have anyone in mind?"

I swatted him. "You know what I mean, Will. I wish your mom was healthier, but considering her age she's done really well."

"Yeah."

"You don't sound convinced."

"When I was sitting at dinner tonight I looked around the table and realized my mother isn't who I've had in my head all these years." Will paused, as if putting the words together from a life span of memories.

"She's all of that, the strong, immovable mountain I've always known as my mama. But she's changed, too. She's more tolerant of the bigger issues, less patient with the little annoyances."

"I hope we all get to where she is, Will. Look at how much she's grown—she was brought up to believe in the black-and-white of life, no pun intended. She's had to adjust to, and I think she's even accepted, the grays. That's quite an accomplishment."

"You know what truly amazes me, Deb?"

I stared into his eyes, the harbor of my heart.

"What's that?"

"You."

"Me?" My stomach dropped a notch. Had my soap-box speech angered him?

"Yes, you. You talk about her coming a long way— you didn't even know 'china' didn't necessarily refer to a country when I met you. You've dealt with prejudiced idiots from all walks of life. Yet you still have the same positive, cheery outlook that you did when I saved you from the school bus over fifty years ago."

"I didn't need any saving! You didn't save me—you watched out for me."

"Whatever you want to call it. I'd like to think I've saved you from yourself, too."

I told myself to calm down and let him talk. This was about Will and his feelings about his mother. But it was difficult to sit still while he turned the conversation toward me.

"What's wrong with me that I needed saving from myself?"

"Nothing. You've just had a chance to relax the strict habits you grew up with."

"I don't know. If we hadn't married I'd still have my degrees, my education. That's not something anyone can take from me."

"No, but you'd still be clipping coupons and stocking up on cans of tuna and tomato soup." Will smiled.

"There's nothing wrong with tuna and soup."

"No, but we can afford healthy, unprocessed food. You said yourself you're grateful you can shop at the organic store instead of the box warehouse."

"Yes, I did."

"And you wouldn't have started shopping there unless I dragged you into a nicer grocery store over thirty years ago."

"I wouldn't go that far..." Will was hitting too close to my emotional jugular. It'd been difficult for me to shift gears from not having much of anything as a child and student, to being able to have whatever I needed, whatever I wanted.

Will sat up and leaned against the pillows on his side of the bed.

"I don't want to fight, honey. You're getting your guard up and I'm sorry I said anything. I just wanted to make the point that I'm happy the women in my life can sit down at the table together, and the love and respect they have for each other shines through."

"Thanks..."

"Come here and give me a kiss."

Not one to argue in bed, I did exactly that.

CHAPTER TWENTY-FIVE

Present Day
Somewhere over the Atlantic

THE FLIGHT WAS MORE comfortable than Angie had
expected. It didn't hurt that Mom and Dad had surprised
her with an upgrade to business class. She stretched out
in the reclining seat and watched her personal television
screen. The movie was a romantic comedy.

Since she had no idea whether her own story would
end happily or tragically she didn't want to get involved
in the movie. She pressed the channel changer and an
animated film appeared.

Even the cartoon cat was pregnant.

Had society always been this family focused, or was
it something she noticed in her current state?

"More tea, miss?"

Angie smiled at the flight attendant. He was probably her age.

"No, thanks. How much longer?"

"We're about halfway."

"Thank you." The flight attendant meant halfway to
Paris. But for Angie, it was halfway home to Jesse.

Present Day
Paris, France

"I NEVER MEANT for our break to be permanent, Angie."

"Me, neither. But when you didn't call, and you didn't offer any resistance to the idea of me transferring to Buffalo, I took that as your answer."

Angie's entire body was on alert as she sat facing Jesse on the park bench. They'd met at the airport as planned, with no delays. Their luggage was already at the hotel, where they'd stopped only to freshen up before venturing out into the Paris streets.

Jesse combed through his hair with his fingers. His wireless glasses did nothing to hide the burning intensity of his blue eyes as he studied her every expression.

"God, Angie." He clasped her hands. "I really messed this up. And I don't want you to think this is a passing phase because I've been around so much death and pain. I've also seen a lot of hope in the kids who pull through."

Angie smiled at him and spoke quietly. "'Kids'? Weren't some of them our age?"

"Yeah, but most were just out of high school, maybe college. That's the one big reason I was able to help so many. If it was you or I with those kind of head injuries..." Jesse's voice trailed off and he looked at the dirt on the park's path. Their bench was to one side, and they had a fantastic view of the Concorde Place from there, including the Egyptian obelisk.

"I'm so sorry, Jesse. It must be really tough on you." She took her right hand from under his and stroked his cheek. He grabbed her hand and pressed her palm to his lips.

Searing awareness charged her hormones, already active thanks to her pregnancy.

She *had* to tell him.

"Angie, I don't want to talk about my work right now. I want to talk about us."

Angie forced back the watery pressure behind her eyes.

Jesse looked at her. "Okay. Let's do it," he said. She knew what *it* would be.

"Oh, Jess—"

"I think we should—"

They both stopped and grinned at each other.

"I'm sorry. You first." She had to give him a chance.

"Angie, we've been—*I've* been—really stupid. I should've considered having a family years ago. You aren't my mother, I'm not my father. We're *us*. I believe in us, and more importantly, these past three months have taught me that I don't want to live without you. I can't—not if I'm going to live the life I'm meant to live."

"Oh, Jesse." Where did she start?

"Wait, this is still my turn, okay?" His expression was serious, his gaze intent. "I need to be with you. I need for us to be a family."

When he uttered the word *family,* Angie felt a tiny flutter deep inside her belly, as though there was a butterfly trapped there. She gasped and put her hand to her abdomen.

"What? Are you having a cramp?"

She laughed. "No, no. Go on."

Jesse looked a little perplexed at her reaction but kept talking.

"I'm not joking about this, Angie. We belong together, and if you can forgive me for being such a hardheaded arse for so long, I want to make it up to you."

She smiled at his use of *arse.* It was a private joke between them from their much-enjoyed trip to Scotland three years ago.

Despite the humorous interjection, there was no doubt that he was serious. But she still wasn't convinced.

"I think we're going too fast. Maybe we should wait until you're back in the States for a few months, and this is well behind you." She knew that people did crazy things in wartime, that they looked for emotional connections and—

"Angie, as far as I'm concerned, we're not going fast enough."

Jessed eased off the bench and reached into his pocket. He pulled out a black velvet ring box as he knelt in front of her.

"Jesse, your—"

"Angela Bradley Medford, will you stay with me forever and be the mother of my children?"

Angie didn't deserve this. After all she'd put them through, all she'd kept from Jesse these past months.

Jesse had never lost faith in her, in their love.

She grasped his hands with hers, covering the ring box with her own hand.

"Yes, Jesse Medford, I'll do whatever you want, my love."

Jesse placed the intricately carved gold ring on Angie's shaking right finger. He kissed the back of her hand and then looked up, into her eyes and straight to her heart.

"When we got married, it was forever, Angie."

"I know, Jesse. I know."

He got to his feet and pulled her up next to him, and Angie didn't care who was watching. It was just the two of them—the *three* of them—and a delicious kiss.

Of course, she still had to tell him about their child.

"Jesse, there's one more thing. Now that you've, um, kind of…proposed to me again, it's only fair to tell you that you haven't been talking just to me."

Jesse frowned with that puzzled expression she adored. "Oh?"

Confidence welled up in her. Love for Jesse and faith that he'd changed. He'd accept her *and* their baby.

"Do you remember the bottle of Barolo on New Year's Eve?"

"Sure, I vaguely remember the bottle of wine. But what I remember clearly is you, naked, on the floor…"

He grew silent and Angie pulled back. His body was still, his face unreadable. He blinked.

"You—we—we're pregnant?"

"Yes." Tears poured down her cheeks. And they weren't due to the hormones.

They came from the joy that exploded inside her at Jesse's huge grin.

He let out a loud "whoop" and pulled her to him, lifting her off the ground and spinning her around. Her ankles hit the wrought-iron legs of the park bench.

"Ow. Jesse!"

"I'm sorry, Angie. But we're going to be a family! Do you know what that means?"

"I have an idea—and I figure we'll find out the rest together."

CHAPTER TWENTY-SIX

Two Weeks Later
Buffalo, New York

WILL CLIMBED the marble steps to the Albright Knox Art Gallery. A cold breeze rose up off the lake and gently buffeted his back. He paused to glance over his shoulder at Delaware Park.

It was a view that probably hadn't changed in nearly a century. The green leaf buds were already visible on all the deciduous trees. The daffodils weren't far behind the crocuses peeking through the remnants of snow.

Conscious of a sense of history, he turned back to the museum. Debra was part of this history, part of *his* history. Her work, which she'd so often relegated to second place behind his and the children's needs, was on display and would reveal to the world what a talent she had.

He smiled to himself. He couldn't wait to see the show.

Debra

"I NEED ONE MORE SPOTLIGHT, in the far right exhibit, over the black-and-white of Martin Luther King."

I spoke on the tiny walkie-talkie to the museum employee who was assigned to me throughout the life of the exhibit.

In fifteen minutes, the doors would open. Tonight was for invited guests—mostly my family, friends, gallery board members and other artists. Tomorrow morning the month-long public exhibit would commence. In four weeks I'd be on the road to Atlanta, then Denver, as the collection toured the country.

"Light's on over the King exhibit, Ms. Bradley. Anything else you need?"

"No, thank you, Jenny." The young art student had done a superb job for me ever since we'd started the set-up the previous weekend.

I needed the last ten minutes to do my usual walk-through before the doors opened. I pressed the button on the walkie-talkie.

"Jen?"

"Yes, Ms. Bradley?"

"Don't open the doors until I meet you out front, okay? I'm going to do one final check."

"Got it. See you in ten."

I smiled. So polite, but still a reminder to be by the entrance in no more than ten minutes. No doubt Jen had worked with enough eccentric and egocentric artists to necessitate the prompt.

I took a deep breath and started my last private tour.

WILL MET ME at the front of the gallery. I smiled at him. The electric jolt that raced down my arms and spine weren't from nerves, but from the awareness that this exhibit meant nothing to me unless it meant everything to him.

"Hi, sweetheart." I walked over and lifted my face for his kiss.

He kissed me and pulled back. "You look fantastic. You are such a beautiful—" he leaned in, his lips against my ear "—sexy—" he straightened "—woman."

"All for you." I grasped his hand. I'd bought the dress just for this evening—a champagne-hued slip, covered with black lace. The sleeveless bodice came in snug at my waist, then flared out in party fashion until the skirt ended just above my knees. Tiny iridescent black bugle beads were sewn all over the skirt and neck edges, adding a festive touch.

I felt as though we were walking in to the wedding reception we'd never had.

"Come on, handsome. I have something to show you." I smiled at the man who was my best friend, my confidant, my lover, my life's mate. He smiled back and my breath was swept away by how gorgeous he looked in the charcoal suit.

"Lead the way."

And so I did. Through the entire display of my work, my art.

But it wasn't just a portfolio of my art, or even of the history of my nation during those years.

It was *our* story.

I'd included all of my most significant fiber art pieces—macrame from the seventies, wall hangings from the eighties, tapestries and weavings from the past few years. But also, mixed in with my actual artwork

I'd included the pieces of my life. Of our life together these past forty-plus years.

I had blown up images of significant historical events from the time we were born in the early 1950s, through the Civil Rights era, the Vietnam War, Watergate, the Buffalo Blizzard of 1977. I took the visitor on a tour of the 1980s and 1990s, through the sorrow of September 11, 2001, up until today.

I included my work from all those times, from each phase of my life.

But what neither Will nor anyone else expected was that I'd personalize it so minutely. I'd included photos of our family, in all its stages, blown up as large as the historical photos.

Because for us, this was *our* life. Our events were as meaningful to us as the national ones.

Will was speechless throughout the tour. He paused at length in front of the picture taken on our wedding day. He, Angie and I in our tiny first apartment.

But what brought my man to tears was the photo I'd had made of Violet and Dr. Bradley, placed next to the V-Day photos taken in downtown Buffalo. Their marriage made Will's life possible, and thus, my life with Will.

The shawl I'd made Violet was displayed here, its tattered fibers obviously worn with love.

"You…you brought my family back together."

"*We* brought your family back together, Will. Our love did." I turned him into my arms. "It's always been us, Will. And you've always been the only man for me."

We stood in each other's arms for a few moments.

The doors would open to the rest of the family and other guests in about three minutes.

"I was so wrong to accuse you of being ashamed of our relationship," he whispered.

"No, you weren't. I was never ashamed of us, Will, but I did feel responsible for whatever way others might treat our kids. I don't anymore. You understand that, don't you?"

"And how." He pressed his forehead to mine, then looked back at the photo of his parents.

"I wish Dad were here."

"He is."

We stayed a bit longer.

"Come here. I have one more thing to show you." I led Will around the corner and we stood, hand in hand, in front of my favorite piece.

The showpiece of the exhibit.

The tapestry hung from the rafters, and took up the better part of the far wall. It wasn't just a weaving of a large tree against the Buffalo skyline. It was our family tree, not emblazoned with names or words, but with seasons, colors, emotions.

"Oh, Debra." Will's voice reflected my heart's song. "This is what it's all about. Family."

My walkie-talkie buzzed.

"Ms. Bradley?"

"Yes, Jen, we're on our way."

"Doors open in one minute."

I looked back up at Will. I knew that Blair, Stella, Brian and Angie were waiting with Violet. Angie had made it back in time from Paris, after all.

Even my mother and Fred had come to see the big event.

But only one opinion mattered to me.

"So what do you think, Will?"

"I think Mama's going to burst with pride. I already am."

"My sweet Will." I kissed him and he responded tenderly, his hands warm on my bare arms.

"The best is yet to come, Debra," he said in a low voice.

"Yes—the best is yet to come." I leaned into him as we looked at our family. Blair had announced Stella's pregnancy a week ago, and their joy was reflected in their wide grins. Brian's new girlfriend, the first he'd ever brought home to meet us, stood at his side. A visibly pregnant Angie was there, too…and looking forward to Jesse's return home, to Buffalo.

Violet sat comfortably in the wheelchair she'd fought against but had given in to once the kids had assured her one of them would stay with her throughout the night. She wore her pearls and a fine silk blouse. Her lap was covered not by a fancy scarf or throw but by the tattered afghan I'd knitted all those years ago.

Will's hand tightened on my waist and I looked up into his beloved face.

"Ready, Deb?"

"Ready."

We turned back toward the family. "Thank you all so much for being here," I said. "I know I would never have come this far without my family. I love you all."

* * * * *

Harlequin is 60 years old,
and Harlequin Blaze is celebrating!
After all, a lot can happen in 60 years,
or 60 minutes…or 60 seconds!
Find out what's going down in Blaze's
heart-stopping new miniseries,
FROM 0 TO 60!
Getting from "Hello" to "How was it?"
can happen fast….

Here's a sneak peek of the first book,
A LONG, HARD RIDE
by Alison Kent.
Available March 2009.

"IS THAT FOR ME?" Trey asked.

Cardin Worth cocked her head to the side and considered how much better the day already seemed. "Good morning to you, too."

When she didn't hold out the second cup of coffee for him to take, he came closer. She sipped from her heavy white mug, hiding her grin and her giddy rush of nerves behind it.

But when he stopped in front of her, she made the mistake of lowering her gaze from his face to the exposed strip of his chest. It was either give him his cup of coffee or bury her nose against him and breathe in. She remembered so clearly how he smelled. How he tasted.

She gave him his coffee.

After taking a quick gulp, he smiled and said, "Good morning, Cardin. I hope the floor wasn't too hard for you."

The hardness of the floor hadn't been the problem. She shook her head. "Are you kidding? I slept like a baby, swaddled in my sleeping bag."

"In my sleeping bag, you mean."

If he wanted to get technical, yeah. "Thanks for the loaner. It made sleeping on the floor almost bearable."

As had the warmth of his spooned body, she thought, then quickly changed the subject. "I saw you have a loaf of bread and some eggs. Would you like me to cook breakfast?"

He lowered his coffee mug slowly, his gaze as warm as the sun on her shoulders, as the ceramic heating her hands. "I didn't bring you out here to wait on me."

"You didn't bring me out here at all. I volunteered to come."

"To help me get ready for the race. Not to serve me."

"It's just breakfast, Trey. And coffee." Even if last night it had been more. Even if the way he was looking at her made her want to climb back into that sleeping bag. "I work much better when my stomach's not growling. I thought it might be the same for you."

"It is, but I'll cook. You made the coffee."

"That's because I can't work at all without caffeine."

"If I'd known that, I would've put on a pot as soon I got up."

"What time *did* you get up?" Judging by the sun's position, she swore it couldn't be any later than seven now. And, yeah, they'd agreed to start working at six.

"Maybe four?" he guessed, giving her a lazy smile.

"But it was almost two…" She let the sentence dangle, finishing the thought privately. She was quite sure he knew exactly what time they'd finally fallen asleep after he'd made love to her.

The question facing her now was where did this relationship—if you could even call it *that*—go from here?

* * * * *

Cardin and Trey are about to find out that
great sex is only the beginning....
Don't miss the fireworks!
Get ready for
A LONG, HARD RIDE
by Alison Kent.
Available March 2009,
wherever Blaze books are sold.

CELEBRATE
60 YEARS
OF PURE READING PLEASURE
WITH HARLEQUIN®!

We'll be spotlighting a different series
every month throughout 2009
to celebrate our 60th anniversary.

Look for Harlequin® Blaze™ in March!

0-60

*After all, a lot can happen in 60 years,
or 60 minutes...or 60 seconds!*

Find out what's going down in Blaze's
heart-stopping new miniseries *0-60!*
Getting from "Hello" to "How was it?"
can happen fast....

Look for the brand-new 0-60 miniseries in March 2009!

www.eHarlequin.com   HBRIDE09

REQUEST YOUR FREE BOOKS!

2 FREE NOVELS PLUS 2 FREE GIFTS!

HARLEQUIN®

Super Romance®

Exciting, emotional, unexpected!

SPECIAL EDITION

TRAVIS'S APPEAL

by *USA TODAY* bestselling author
MARIE FERRARELLA

Shana O'Reilly couldn't deny it—family lawyer
Travis Marlowe had some kind of appeal. But
as Travis handled her father's tricky estate
planning, he discovered things weren't what
they seemed in the O'Reilly clan. Would
an explosive secret leave Travis and Shana's
budding relationship in tatters?

*Available March 2009
wherever books are sold.*

The Inside Romance newsletter has a NEW look for the new year!

Same great content, brand-new look!

The Inside Romance newsletter is a FREE quarterly newsletter highlighting our upcoming series releases and promotions!

Click on the Inside Romance link on the front page of **www.eHarlequin.com** or e-mail us at insideromance@harlequin.ca to sign up to receive your FREE newsletter today!

You can also subscribe by writing to us at: HARLEQUIN BOOKS Attention: Customer Service Department P.O. Box 9057, Buffalo, NY 14269-9057

Please allow 4-6 weeks for delivery of the first issue by mail.

IRNNEW09

HARLEQUIN®

Super Romance®

COMING NEXT MONTH

Available March 10, 2009

BUNDLES of JOY

#1548 MOTHER TO BE • Tanya Michaels
9 Months Later
With a sizzling career in commercial real estate and an even hotter younger
boyfriend, Delia Carlisle can't believe those two pink lines of a pregnancy test
are real. She's forty-three, for Pete's sake! Suddenly Delia's not just giving birth
to a baby—*everything* in her life is about to change....

#1549 CHILD'S PLAY • Cindi Myers
You, Me & the Kids
Designer Diana Shelton is not what principal Jason Benton expects when he
commissions a playscape for his school. Even though he falls instantly for her—
pregnancy and all—getting involved complicates this single dad's life...until he
discovers love can be as simple as child's play.

#1550 SOPHIE'S SECRET • Tara Taylor Quinn
Shelter Valley Stories
For years Duane Konch and Sophie Curtis have had a secret affair. That works
for them—given their difference in ages and his social status. Then Sophie gets
pregnant. And now she must choose between the man she loves and the child
they've created.

#1551 A NATURAL FATHER • Sarah Mayberry
Single, pregnant and in need of a business partner is not what Lucy Basso
had planned. Still, things look up when hottie Dominic Bianco invests in her
company. It's just too bad she can't keep her mind *on* business and *off* thoughts
of how great a father he might be.

#1552 HER BEST FRIEND'S BROTHER • Kay Stockham
The Tulanes of Tennessee
Pregnant by her best friend's brother? No, this isn't happening to Shelby Brookes.
That crazy—unforgettable—night with Luke Tulane was their little secret. But
no way can it remain a secret now. Not with Luke insisting they meet at the altar
in front of everyone!

#1553 BABY IN HER ARMS • Stella MacLean
Everlasting Love
Widow Emily Martin loves having a newborn in her arms—her own babies in
the past and now her grandchild. It's all about new life...although that's a phrase
she's been hearing far too often from her children, who say *she* needs to start
living again. And then she finds eleven love letters from her husband....

HSRCNMBPA0209